Gold Medal Summer

Donna Freitas

SCHOLASTIC INC.

No part of this publication may be reproduced, stored in a retrieval system, or transmitted in any form or by any means, electronic, mechanical, photocopying, recording, or otherwise, without written permission of the publisher. For information regarding permission, write to Scholastic Inc., Attention: Permissions Department, 557 Broadway, New York, NY 10012.

ISBN 978-0-545-32789-3

Text copyright © 2012 by Donna Freitas. Illustrations © 2012 by Kyle T. Webster. All rights reserved. Published by Scholastic Inc. SCHOLASTIC, the LANTERN LOGO, and associated logos are trademarks and/or registered trademarks of Scholastic Inc.

Arthur A. Levine Books hardcover edition designed by Elizabeth B. Parisi, published by Arthur A. Levine Books, an imprint of Scholastic Inc., June 2012.

12 11 10 9 8 7 6 5 4 3 2 1   14 15 16 17 18 19/0

Printed in the U.S.A. 40
This edition first printing, May 2014

To Cheryl Klein,

for about a million different reasons.

Front Walkover

Back   *Handspring*

Back Layout

Front Tuck

Press-to Handstand

Yurchenko

Cast Handstand

Kip

Don't be afraid if things seem difficult in the beginning.

That's only the initial impression.

The important thing is not to retreat;

you have to master yourself.

— OLGA KORBUT, USSR,

four-time Olympic gold medalist in 1972 and 1976

I've never understood why people cry on the podium.

Why, after winning gold at a gymnastics meet, in the middle of all that glory, there are tears and not plain, simple happiness.

When I think about the different girls I've watched step up to take their place at the very top spot, receiving flowers and waving at the cheering crowd, I can't help but wonder how many of them cry crocodile tears, faking emotion because that's what people expect, or because it makes for a better photo opp.

Take Sarah Walker of the Jamestown Gymcats. She's the best tumbler in the state, but she's better known for chewing out teammates in public than for her double twist into a punch front tuck on floor. Then there's Jennifer Adams, probably the biggest standout on the uneven parallel bars Rhode Island has seen in a decade. But she shrieks at the top of her lungs during rivals' routines to psych them out, just before someone dismounts from the beam or starts her run for the vault. Jennifer Adams is merciless. Not to mention without class.

Put Sarah or Jennifer in that number one spot, though, and tears automatically fall.

I don't get it.

Then again, it's never been me up there.

It's not that I don't want it as badly as the other girls. Believe me, I do. I want gold so much I'd eat it for breakfast if it would make a difference. Sprinkle it on my spaghetti like Parmesan cheese and pour it over my ice cream like it's hot fudge. I'd even coat myself head to toe in gold paint if it meant getting to march up to that number one spot and duck my head so the judge can drape that medal around my neck.

If gold medal glory *does* ever happen to me, Joey Jordan of the Gansett Stars, lover of beam and floor, hater of the vault, proud wearer of a sparkly leotard, tears will not be on the menu that day. I'll be smiling as big as ever up on that podium.

I promise.

That's just who I am.

CHAPTER ONE

Nearly perfect isn't enough.

Step, step, pirouette. Pose. Hand flick.

Come on, Joey, next comes your favorite move on beam, the handstand you hold forever, that ends with the split that shows off your flexibility and style, which helps the judges forget you do a round off into a boring back layout instead of a full twist for your dismount. . . .

"Go, Joey," I hear my best friend, Alex, call from my right.

I flick my hands again for her benefit and, well, the judges' too, and kick my handstand in a way that demonstrates my ability to easily achieve a perfect split on the way up. The slight tug this creates along the length of my muscles is satisfying because of the way it pushes the limits of my flexibility, and I love knowing it turns the shape of my body into something worthy of awe.

"Ooohh," the audience sighs, their appreciation audible even over the Tchaikovsky playing for a competitor's floor exercise.

Both hands grip the edge of the beam, the heels of my palms holding my balance, every muscle in my body tight, toes so pointed they form a capital C. One knee bends toward my head, the other sends my toes toward the ceiling. After nailing the pose, I shift my legs into a straddle split until they are parallel to the beam. Then, ever so slowly, my shoulders pressing forward, my stomach muscles screaming with the strain, I lower my body until that split hovers just inches over the apparatus. I hold it extra long, long enough that I hear "wows" rippling through the crowd. A gymnast like me has to impress the judges with this kind of move, and I know Judge Garrison will count exactly how many seconds I stay in this position. These poses are her favorite, and she rewards gymnasts who can pull stuff like this off. To come out of it, I swivel so each leg is perpendicular to the beam, swing myself up to a standing position, and then walk — albeit with poise and style and a few flashy smiles — to the other end.

Now comes the part I hate.

There's this series of moves I'm terrible at but it's in my routine regardless — a back handspring, back handspring into a back layout. Coach Angelo says I need a sequence like this with a high degree of difficulty that is worth a lot of points, but I almost never stick it, so it ruins my score anyway.

A single fall drops your score an entire point. Gold medal hopes dashed in less than a second. *Poof.* Just. Like. That.

"Concentrate, Joey, concentrate," Coach says from the sidelines, where he's watching and evaluating every detail.

"She totally won't make this. She *always* falls," I hear Sarah Walker say.

Take your time, Joey, I reassure myself and breathe deep. Wish for the sort of superhuman focus that blocks everything out, the kind that sorts the gymnasts who win at competitions from those who don't. I need to erase the presence of my coach and Alex and especially Sarah, my biggest rival on beam. I do have one advantage over Sarah, though. She goes through routines like they're a series of drills, with no artistry or joy. I don't think she's ever even smiled during her floor or beam routine. She totally lacks style.

But me, I'm all smiles, even as dread fills the empty space in my stomach.

I do my best to shake off the fear and frustration, flicking my chin upward, throwing my shoulders back, extending my arms forward so the tips of my fingers are my only focus, everything around them, behind them, the area for the vault, the thick mats at the end of the beam, all of it becoming a blur.

I can do this. I *will* do this.

"That's it, Joey! That's it. You've got it in you," Coach cheers softly.

But as I rise on my toes, my arms poised to swing behind me, about to throw myself into the first back handspring, Sarah Walker says, "Joey Jordan is all style and no substance," like she's just visited the inside of my brain and heard my every thought. I falter a moment, enough that I'm suddenly off balance the very second my body gains momentum for the first flip-flop. My foot shifts, then slips slightly, but I keep going anyway — I have to, I need to stick this pass to win — so I stretch straight on up into the second back handspring, my eyes spotting the beam as my legs travel over my head.

It's not enough, though. Not enough, because after all this work, psyching myself up and out and up again, my foot catches weirdly on the landing, and my arms are suddenly flailing, balance gone, and I crash into a heap of long, skinny limbs, bright against the royal blue mats.

"Awwwww," comes the disappointment from the crowd.

"I knew she'd choke," says Sarah Walker.

"Pathetic," one of her teammates adds and they let go into a fit of loud, squealing giggles.

"Get up," Coach says from my left, loud enough that his judgment booms through my brain. "Joey, get up. Finish like a champion. Do it. Now!"

"Come on, Joey," Alex says.

Shaking, breathing hard with tiny, short pushes from my lungs, I untangle my arms and legs and pull myself up until I can stand and walk back over to the beam. Both hands hover a moment above the scratchy, padded covering, and I feel the heat pouring from my palms, causing the rip I got earlier today on bars to burn. When I'm finally ready, I hop up and position myself at one end, trying to act like nothing happened, like I didn't just fall and wreck my hopes for gold today, like my entire body isn't still tingling with fear. I do a couple of hand flicks that aren't in my routine and not only skip the back layout that by now there is no way I would land, but I even avoid the dismount I am supposed to do because I'm too shaky to manage it. Instead, I turn around and throw a simple back tuck off the side of the beam, doing my best to recover some sort of composure after my humiliating fall.

Made all the more humiliating because just moments ago, I'd nearly stuck a perfect routine.

My landing is solid and I throw my arms back past my ears for the crowd and judges, because this is what you do no matter what, even if you crash ten times. I step to the side to smile, pose again to signal my finish, and begin the requisite gymnast's prance toward my teammates. But as soon as I turn away, the smile on my face disappears. If only Coach would allow me to do a routine that I excel at, one with moves better-suited to my strengths, then maybe I would finally stick beam at a competition for once.

"It's okay," Alex says the second I am close enough to hear. "Aside from the last tumbling pass and your dismount" — notice how she doesn't say *fall*? — "you were perfect. Seriously. You'll still medal, Joey. Maybe even silver."

I appreciate the way Alex is always the wishful thinker when it comes to my medal potential, even though she's usually wrong.

I was the last competitor to finish today, so everyone is already gathering by the podium in the middle of the floor exercise. I don't have long before I find out that, yes, even though I got only an 8.2, I did indeed medal for beam.

Bronze. Not silver, but bronze.

"It's just too bad you don't have the height for your flips," Sarah Walker hisses above me, her gold medal catching the late afternoon sunlight streaming through the window. "You do look so *sweet* doing that little routine of yours, though."

I am stone, I am stone, I repeat to myself, willing my mouth into a tight line so I don't bark back, my feet firm on the lowest podium. My bronze is dull and looks almost dirty.

It's fitting, I suppose. Placing third *is* dull. Simple as that.

"Now for the winners of the All-Around," the announcer says, signaling that it's time for the three of us to head back to our respective teams, which have gathered in small crowds nearby. A part of me wants to walk straight by my coaches and teammates and on out the door, since I probably didn't even crack the top five this meet and don't really feel like suffering more disappointment today, but I don't.

"Nice job on beam, Joey," says my teammate Trish, giving me a quick hug and a smile that is thoroughly genuine. Trish is one of the nicest girls at our gym, and she's drop-dead gorgeous too. We're allowed to wear makeup at competitions, but Trish doesn't need any. It's easy to forgive her looks when she treats everyone with such kindness.

Well, that, and she never wins any medals.

I thank Trish, then take my usual place at Alex's side. The announcer says the name of the bronze winner into the microphone — Jennifer Adams — and I try not to gag. Alex looks at me, her face white, and I ask, "Are you ready to be a star or what?"

Alex shifts from one foot to the other, her eyes downcast like she's placed last and not won the entire competition. "I'm not a star," she says. "Stop saying stuff like that."

"I only said it because it's true. Besides, 'We're *all* stars,'" I add with a roll of my eyes, trying to make her smile. Coach Angelo is constantly telling us this, since our team is called the Gansett Stars.

Alex starts to protest further, but stops short because her name booms from the speakers as the winner of today's gold medal for All-Around. I squeeze her hand quickly, watching as her head snaps up and she forces a smile to her lips. She walks forward, waving at the crowd. The cheers for her are deafening.

She's such an audience favorite. I wonder if I'm the only person close enough to see that her smile never makes it to her eyes, that even after winning the whole day, there is intense sadness written all over her face.

After Alex climbs to the top, she drops her head so one of the judges can loop a red-white-and-blue-striped ribbon around her neck, the one with that coveted gold medallion dangling at the end of it. Alex looks up again, and I see them there, just like always.

Tears.

When Alex smiles, they spill from her eyes, the pressure from her cheeks tipping tiny lakes down her face, leaving streaks across her skin. The crowd thinks these are tears of joy, but I know better. The tears are because her ankle hurts and she competed through the pain today, because yet another win will get her even more and harsher attention from Coach at practice tomorrow. Because she's tired of being a gymnast, plain and simple. Alex keeps saying she's going to quit, and I'm beginning to believe she might be serious.

When the medal ceremony is over, I head toward the place I left my warm-ups and bag this morning, when the promise of a win was still ahead. Thinking about the hopes I had only hours ago brings tears to my eyes too.

"Joey," Alex calls after me, her quick, soft footsteps approaching.

For a split second I want to snap at her, even though she has never been anything but the best of best friends. But sometimes, it's hard to have a best friend who's so miserable she couldn't care less about winning, and even so, wins every time.

"Are you okay?" she asks me. "Do you want a ride home?"

"I'm fine," I manage, my throat dry. Quickly, I force a smile and pull Alex into a hug, kissing her cheek too. A streak of wet glimmers on her face — whether from her tears or mine, I can't tell. Alex wipes it away, not saying a word, but her eyes are sad again. "Thanks for the offer, but my sister is waiting outside."

"Okay. Well, see you at practice tomorrow, then?"

"Yeah. Where else would I be?" I say, hoisting my gym bag over my shoulder. "Bye, Zany," I add, using Alex's nickname from when we were little and first became friends, watching as she walks out, her ponytail swinging left and right behind her. I'm about to follow, but I can't resist glancing one more time at the podium.

Maybe, just maybe, someday it will be me up there wearing gold, mustering fake tears of joy instead of hiding real tears of defeat. Maybe, just maybe, I'll get the chance to test whether I might smile in that winner's spot instead of cry.

I take a deep breath, straighten up, and put on a brave face as I push through the heavy doors of the gym into the glaring sunlight of the afternoon.

CHAPTER TWO

Sisterly words of wisdom.

"*There* will be other chances to win, Joey," says Julia, with a combination of sympathy and that *buck up, kid* tone I'm used to from years of my sister's pep talks. Her friend Madison nods authoritatively beside her. Julia glances right for traffic, her long blond hair waving across her right shoulder from the movement, then pulls out of the parking lot. "There is *always* a next time," she continues.

"Yeah, well, I wanted it to be *this* time," I say from the backseat of the car, where I'm sulking, I admit it. I may not be a gold medal champion, but I am a champion sulker for sure.

Julia's eyes roll in the rearview mirror. "Gymnastics is not the only thing that matters in life."

"Says the girl who gave up her chance at Olympic gold," I mutter under my breath. When Julia competed for the Gansett Stars, she was the classic power gymnast, tiny, but muscular enough to make any guy athlete seethe with envy. She could reach the kind of height on her tumbling passes and vaults that made a crowd's jaws drop. I'm more of an artistic gymnast, relying on poise, dancing, and flexibility, and the kind of style and emotion that make a crowd clap along with my floor music. If I could trade types with Julia, I would in a heartbeat.

"What was it like back when you competed anyway?" Madison asks my sister.

She shakes her head *no*, as if I'm not going to notice.

"Go ahead, Julia," I sigh, slumping farther down into the seat. "You can tell her."

Madison looks back at me guiltily. "Oh. I didn't mean to —"

"Really, I don't care," I lie.

Julia grabs a bottle of water from the cup holder and takes a swig, her eyes never leaving the road. "Honestly, I can't even remember, it was so long ago. I've been retired almost five years."

"But don't most gymnasts compete in college?" Madison asks.

Julia shrugs. "It's complicated."

Since she won't tell the story and Madison obviously wants all the gory details, I lean forward to weigh in on my sister's meteoric rise to gymnastics glory. "Yeah, Julia won more gold medals than she could count, and then she decided to go out on top after she became National Champion at age sixteen."

"Joey," my sister says, twisting around to look at me while we wait at a red light. "That's not the whole story and you know it. I did not *decide* to go out on top."

My turn to shrug. I stare out the window at the little café to our left, as well as the ice cream shop and the diner across the road where Alex and I go sometimes after practice. Not that we have much time to enjoy any of it.

"By the time I was competing at Nationals, I was injured," Julia goes on. "Badly. An ACL torn beyond repair. And injuries are the number one reason why any gymnast retires."

I can't resist commenting. "But you *won* Nationals," I say. The seat belt cuts across me, straining to yank me back. "You could have come back from the injury and you *chose* not to. You had a shot at Olympic gold, and you didn't retire. You *quit*." This last word I whisper, so taboo in the world of gymnastics that you almost never risk saying it aloud. Its hushed sound hangs in the air. I know I am not being nice and sympathetic to Julia like she is being to me, but sometimes having a superstar older sister makes you say mean things.

Julia meets my remarks with a long silence. Slowly, I return to my slouch in the backseat, wishing I could disappear like a wizard, or one of those people with magic rings that make them invisible.

"Um," Madison says awkwardly. "Sorry to bring up a sore subject."

Julia flicks her hair from her right shoulder to her left. "Don't worry about it. Ever since Joey got serious about gymnastics, she's had a difficult time understanding my decision to *retire*."

My eyes are glued to the window and I play with the button that opens it. "I'm right here, you know. Listening to every word."

Julia ignores me. "Like she said, I won Nationals when I was sixteen," she says, while navigating the windy, pothole-ridden street that leads out of the town center.

I resist clapping my hands against my ears to block out Julia's voice. It is almost too painful to listen.

"It was thrilling," Julia goes on. "Truly. But the thing about gymnastics is that the better *you* get, the worse everything about being in the sport gets. Once you are at the point where you are competing at meets like Regionals and Nationals, your skill level needs to be really high. The higher the skill level, the more difficult everything is physically, sure, but even worse is how difficult it all gets emotionally. Gymnasts develop fears about certain moves and get hang-ups about doing routines at meets or anxiety about certain rivals who can psych them out. And all those fears and hang-ups and anxieties, they not only put a damper on how you feel about what you are doing, but they can put you in danger too. Fear makes you weak, and weakness gets you injured. It's kind of ironic, right? The better you become, the less you love doing gymnastics."

Yup, I'm thinking in the backseat. I can totally relate to all of the above. But even though I'm smarting about my disappointing loss today, I know I'm like the opposite of Alex. The more she wins, the more her love of the sport disappears, and the more I *don't quite* win, the more badly I want to realize my dream.

"So there I am, up on the podium, listening as they play the national anthem, and I've got the gold medal hanging around my neck, my dream come true. But even though I was happy in that one moment, my body was in so much pain — because that's what gymnasts do, you know? They compete through the pain. Somehow everything I'd done to get to that place, all the years nursing injuries and working through the psychological hurdles and training without having any sort of a social life, and never seeing my friends and family or having a boyfriend, just literally having gymnastics as my entire life and nothing else — all that stuff was up there with me too."

"That's kind of intense," Madison says.

"It was. But even more intense was the idea of trading any more of my life and maybe permanent injuries to my body for this one spot on the podium. And that was it. I knew right then I was done. That I'd just competed for the last time and I'd walk away a national champion, and this one moment would have to be enough." Julia sighs, her eyes on me in the rearview mirror. "The moral of the story, Joey, is that the sacrifices aren't always worth it in the end. I gave up *so* much. And as much as I want you to win gold too, sometimes I hate watching you follow the same path."

"It's not your decision which path I follow," I say, not quite loud enough for Julia to hear.

"I think it's amazingly mature you made that decision," Madison says. Everyone feels this way about Julia. "I can't believe you never talk about it. I mean, at school, it's like you were never a gymnast at all."

"Yeah, well, it's a long time ago. And I have a very different life now. A life I really love. And friends I really love —"

"And boys you really love," Madison whispers with a laugh.

"I have no regrets," Julia says. "And Mom and Dad practically threw a party for the entire town when I told them I was done. They were so relieved."

Madison turns to face me in the backseat. "Joey, you're thirteen, right?"

"I'll be fourteen by the beginning of next school year," I respond. "In September."

"That means you have exactly two years and two months before you get to retire too," she says and laughs.

"Madison," Julia says in a low voice. "Don't."

"Oh, um, well," Madison stammers. "Joey, I'm sure you have a long career ahead of you as a gymnast —"

"No, really, it's okay," I say, my voice angry and frustrated. "I'm used to being reminded that I'll never catch up to my sister's success — that I'll never be as good as Julia. She could always impress the judges with her power and her tumbling, and that's why she won and I never will."

"Oh, Joey," Julia says, swinging the car left into our driveway. "Today is just one bad day."

The second she stops the car, I'm going to get out.

As if she knows I'm waiting, she slows the car to a crawl so she can fit in a few more words of so-called wisdom. "And there's more than one way to impress people," she says, finally turning the key so everything goes quiet. "It's not just tumbling. You *know* that."

"Tell that to the judges," I say, opening and slamming the car door. My bag bumps against my hip as I cross the front lawn, head held high, shoulders back, chin up, chest out. Even as the posture mantra scrolls through my mind, everything about me feels hunched and curled and slumped, my feet dragging the ground with every step. Another car door slams and then another. I can feel my sister and Madison watching me as I open the screen door. Julia says one last thing just before I get inside.

"You have to *show* them what they're missing, Joey," she calls as the screen bangs closed behind me.

CHAPTER THREE

Mom tries so hard.

"**Joey,** is that you?"

"Yes, Mom," I call back, wanting to escape up the stairs to the parent-free quiet of my room.

"How did it go?" she asks, appearing from around the corner where she's obviously been working in her studio. Paint of all colors is slashed and dotted across her jeans and T-shirt, while most of her auburn hair is gathered up into a ponytail, wisps escaping here and there to frame her face.

"Hey, Mom," Julia says, zipping by us with Madison right behind her. They head through the family room straight out to the backyard and the swimming pool.

"Hi, sweetheart," Mom says without breaking her stare on me.

"The meet was fine," I say, because what other choice do I have? She's not letting me go anywhere without a conversation. "Are you having a good painting day? Feeling inspired?"

"As a matter of fact, yes. But you're not changing the subject that easily. Tell me." She sounds enthusiastic, though I can hear the worry layered underneath her sunny tone. "How did your beam routine go? Did you stick it?"

Any other day, hearing Mom say *stick it* would send my eyes rolling, but today her question simply stings. "Hang on," I tell her and make a left into the kitchen to get some fluids in me. I don't want to dehydrate, and getting a glass of water gives me a little more time to avoid her questions.

Mom and Dad pretty much exhausted their ability to watch gymnastics with Julia. Seeing her compete injured just about killed Mom, and while Dad had more of a stomach for the situation, the way Coach Angelo always pushed Julia, despite the pain, eventually sent him over the edge too. After she retired and I wanted to pursue my own gymnastics dreams, my parents made a deal with me: They would pay the bills, of which there were many; and they would outfit me in whatever I needed. Otherwise, they were out. Mom can't sit through a meet without experiencing serious anxiety and constantly wondering things like, *Is my youngest daughter all in one piece?* And Dad can't control his urge to yell at Coach.

So I go it alone. Mostly.

I get it. I mean, I understand my parents' rationale. Sometimes, I even believe I'm better off without them watching at every meet, especially when I see the stage moms and dads traumatizing my teammates and competition. But occasionally, I wish Mom and Dad could handle themselves better and just come out and be supportive. I want them to see me shine, the way I smile when beam is going just right and how I flirt with the crowd on floor and they eat everything I give them right up. Though, as my parents often remind me, they are *really* supportive on the financial front, and I am lucky that my mother is as crazy successful as she is with her art. Selling one painting can usually pay for an entire year of gymnastics, and she sells way more than one a year.

After popping a couple of ice cubes into a Slurpee-sized plastic cup I find hiding behind some coffee mugs, and filling it at the sink, I down a third of it, my body so thirsty for water I can't stop myself from chugging. Then I take a deep breath, readying myself to chat with Mom. She always wants the play-by-play after the fact, as if this makes up for her absence.

When I come around the corner, I see her settled on the wood floor of the living room, sitting cross-legged by the opened sliding glass door to the deck. A warm breeze coasts through the screen, making everything smell like summer.

I say, "If you must know, and to sum up, my beam routine was a disaster. I fell."

Mom's brow furrows with concern. She doesn't say a word,

though. Just pats the floor next to her, inviting me to sit, waiting patiently for me to go on.

After setting my cup on the coffee table, I peel off my warm-up jacket, throwing it over the arm of the couch. I slide into a straddle split, the skin on the balls of my feet squeaking against the wood on the way down, leaving enough room between Mom and me so I can lay my body flat against the floor for a moment and feel the satisfying stretch in the muscles along the length of my legs. The sound of Julia and Madison gossiping and splashing in the pool travels through the open door, along with the breeze that runs across my skin. I close my eyes, but as soon as I do, I picture the beam, my left foot slipping and skidding down the side and my body crumpling to the mat.

I don't want to see this image again. That's how hang-ups and fears are born. I sit up again and focus on calming my breathing. From the way my mother is staring at me, I know she's mentally sketching me sitting effortlessly in a way that for ordinary humans amounts to contortionist activity. Mom once did an entire series of gymnastics paintings featuring Julia. They practically flew out of the gallery. She's never painted me, though.

"Okay," I say. "My back layout landed me on the mat instead of the beam. Simple as that." Notice how I simplify what happened? It's best not to overdramatize things with my parents.

"Oh, sweetie," she says, her gaze shifting back to that of a concerned mom. "Are you okay?"

She means mentally *and* physically, I know. "Yeah. I'm fine, I guess."

"But you're not. I can tell."

"No. Really. It wasn't a big deal."

"What do you think happened?"

"It's the same old story. I choked."

"Do you want to talk about it?"

I lean forward enough to set my elbows on the floor and rest my chin on my hands. "Not really. Coach will be sure to exhaust the issue tomorrow at practice, so I think I'll take a pass right now."

"Angelo is so harsh on you —"

"On the bright side," I cut in before Mom can go off on a tirade about Coach, "my All-Around score qualified me for Regionals in August. Alex and I are both going — she won the gold for All-Around today, actually."

"Honey, that's great! I'm so happy that you'll have such good company at Regionals. Competitions like that place so much pressure on you girls. You need each other for support."

Translation: Mom hopes that because Alex and I will go to Regionals together, she will be exempt from attending. Winning Regionals automatically qualifies you to compete at

Nationals. In other words, it's a big deal, which means I get to make Mom go if I decide I want her there.

These thoughts are interrupted by Dad's return from his daily run. His sneakers squeak against the floor.

"How's our little champion?" he asks with cheeriness that even a five-year-old would know is fake.

"Not so much a champion as a bronze medalist on beam," I say. My slide backward does not dissuade my father from giving me a sweaty hug.

"Well, that's not so bad, Chewy," he says, using the nickname I wish he would forget. When I was little, *Joey* was apparently too difficult for me, so it came out sounding like *Chewy* when I said it.

"Joey qualified for Regionals today," Mom says.

"Oh goody," Dad says under his breath, but I hear it. "That's great news. Hey, look at your sister. She's having a great time out there with her friend."

"I'm sure Julia is having a very nice time, Dad," I say, my tone sugary sweet.

"You know, you could spend all summer swimming in the pool if you'd just —"

"Mark," Mom interrupts, her voice filled with warning, since Dad is verging on the Quitting Gymnastics speech he gives at least once every few months. "Joey is old enough to make her own decisions."

"Well, Joey needs to think about her future too —"

"Really, Mark. We can have this talk another time."

This is my cue to go upstairs. I'm up from the floor in a flash, grabbing my warm-up jacket from the couch before Dad can say another word.

"Joey!" my mother says, trying to get me to stay, but I'm already rounding the corner.

As I take the stairs two at a time, I remind myself that tomorrow is another day. If I stop at the beach in the morning before practice, I'll be sure to have better luck with my dismount on beam. It's my summer ritual to spend time in the ocean and on the sand before I'm off to six straight hours of nonstop working out. The beach always calms me.

Besides, if I *don't* go, I'll have a terrible practice for sure. That's my deal with the gymnastics gods or the powers that be or whatever you want to call the forces of the universe: If I hang out at the beach in the morning, I'll do great that day, and if I don't make time for it, I'll fall from every event and probably break a leg and an arm too.

Maybe that sounds superstitious. If it does, it's because when it comes to gymnastics, I *am* superstitious.

We all are.

Gymnasts can't help it. It's in our nature.

After dinner that night, I spend an hour online reading

International Gymnast, the magazine bible of all things gymnastics. Then, before I go to bed, I kiss the palm of my hand and tap each of the posters with my favorite Olympic champion gymnasts — Nadia Comaneci, of course, Dominique Dawes, Nastia Liukin, and Ecaterina Szabo.

"Come on, ladies," I tell them. "Lend me your magic."

CHAPTER FOUR

Workout interrupted.

The beach is perfect this morning. The sun is a big yellow ball hovering against the blue, making the ocean glitter below it. A slight breeze cuts the heat. The sand is almost completely empty of bathers, which is just the way I like it.

This bodes well for practice today, I think, as I start a series of sprints up and down the wet, hard sand. *And after yesterday, I need all the help I can get.* The sound of the waves makes me feel so centered, so like myself, like nothing can shake me. If only Regionals took place at the beach, I'd be golden. Maybe literally.

When I finish the sprints, I take a break and walk down to the water. Tiny waves splash across my feet and feel like heaven after all that exertion. I decide to allow myself a few minutes of fun, and spend it cartwheeling in water shin deep, loving the way my toes kick up spray on their way over my head and how my arms are submerged to my elbows. My ponytail dips under and then cools the back of my neck when I'm upright again.

Doing gymnastics at the beach, even simple cartwheels, always helps remind me why I love the sport and why I work so hard day in and day out. Without Coach breathing down my neck, or anyone else to please for that matter, I just enjoy the things my body can do for what they are. Tumbling in the waves is just an added bonus.

After enough cartwheels to coat my skin thoroughly in beads of salt water, I do a few aerials, starting ankle deep, my head easily clearing the water, then moving farther and farther in until during one aerial, my nose barely misses the surf and I almost collapse into the waves, laughing. Then I remember my workout.

I head back up to my towel and dry off. After dropping a stopwatch onto one of my flip-flops, I kick a handstand and stay still as long as I can before I have to hand walk a bit, a few steps left, then a few right. I shift a little more, muscles tight, toes pointed, briefly noticing a perfect, white shell centered between my hands, the size of a dime and so thin I can see through it. The watch ticks toward six minutes, my goal.

There is nothing like being upside down. If you are me, at least.

"Do you *ever* stop for a breath?"

The voice comes suddenly from above and behind me. I do a half turn, the heels of my hands digging into the sand. There are two minutes and twenty-five seconds still remaining, and I'm not about to let someone mess with my workout.

"Excuse me?" I call out without coming down, my eyes searching the beach for the owner of the voice. The *boy* owner. Then I find the feet, then knees, then shoulders, and finally the face of a boy with light curly hair hanging down across his eyes. Still on my hands, I walk a few paces farther away for a better look.

Uh-oh. He's cute. *Really* cute.

Why's he talking to me anyway?

The boy crosses his arms. Looks smug. "I can wait until you're done."

"Um, am I missing something here?" My voice is strained as I do my best not to fall. My shoulders are burning up. "Do I know you?"

"Are you planning to have a conversation with me upside down?"

"No one told me about any conversations scheduled for this morning." Each word requires tremendous effort now. "Please, just give me a sec." Well, forty to be exact. I watch the final seconds on the stopwatch count down to zero, eager to take a break, though not as eager to have to face this boy when I'm upright. *Ten, nine, eight.* I mean, I don't talk to boys on a regular basis. *Five, four.* Who has time for learning *that* skill when you're training? Besides, Coach Angelo forbids us from getting involved with boys. Too much distraction. If only I was a tiny sand crab and I could scuttle away into my tunnel to hide from this situation. Alas.

Zero appears on the stopwatch, and I can finally come down. "Look out," I say. My legs slice the air into a split, then my first leg begins its journey toward the sand, my back arching into a front walkover. One foot lands, the other joins it, and standing again, I turn to see the boy.

"You are very focused," he says.

My breath comes in gasps. "I'm a gymnast," I declare, then feel like an idiot saying this to some random boy. See, it's proven: no boy-talking skills or experience to speak of in my repertoire.

He's a good six inches taller than me, and even cuter now that I'm no longer upside down. He's smiling too — one of those smiles that shows all your teeth, the same kind I use when I perform at competitions.

"The beach is for hanging out and having fun," he says, "not for concentrating."

"Maybe for some people," I say and roll my head in a circle to work out a kink in my neck. Then I shake out my arms and legs, trying to relieve my sore muscles.

The boy brushes his hair out of his eyes and I see that they are big and blue. "You don't remember me, do you?"

I study his face. Rack my brain. "Should I?"

His smile turns into a grin. "Well, I remember you."

"Are you going to make me guess?"

"Come on, think," he says, pausing and tapping a finger against his lips. "My hair used to be *really* blond, practically white in summer. . . ."

My eyes narrow. White blond hair?

"The last time we saw each other, you said you didn't think you could make it a week without seeing me. You were upside down then too, on the monkey bars in Oceanside Park. Joey Jordan," he adds, drawing out each syllable of my name long and slow.

No. Way.

"T. J. Hughes? Is that you?"

"Jackpot," he says and grins again. "Though I go by Tanner now, not T.J. Are you still Joey or are you Johanna these days?"

"No. Never Johanna. Just Joey," I say, seeing the resemblance now. The wide blue eyes, and the blond hair that yes, used to be white and is darker now, but still long and everywhere, and that grin . . . The grin is what jogs my memory most. "I can't believe this. I can't believe it's really you!" I take a step forward, then stop. Are we supposed to hug? Even though I hug my teammates dozens of times in a single practice, somehow, hugging T.J., *Tanner*, feels like a big deal. "It's been, what, like, four years?"

"Five," he says. "I was almost ten and you were almost nine."

"And our birthdays are on the same day, exactly one year apart," I say, laughing as everything starts to come back. "Which was how we became friends in the first place, because our moms decided we should share a birthday party."

"When I was turning eight and you were turning seven."

"They said it was more economical that way."

"And really it was just a disaster."

"Because I wanted a gymnastics party and you wanted a baseball party, and all of my friends used the baseball diamond for the floor exercise." I put my hand over my mouth, laughing harder now.

"My friend Jason hit your friend Sam in the back when he bunted —"

"And I kicked you in the head when you wouldn't get out of my way. Not intentionally, of course. I was doing a back walkover."

He laughs. "So times haven't changed much, then, have they?"

"Not really. Though I'm even more serious about gymnastics now than I was before. It's pretty much my life."

"I figured, from what I've seen online. Your friend — what's her name, Alex? — may take the gold a lot, but it's you in all the photographs. The reporters love describing you on beam."

My cheeks begin to burn. "You've read about me?"

"Obviously," he says.

I don't say anything this time. I don't know what to say. I think this might be what normal girls call flirting. This is not exactly the simple morning workout I had planned.

"So what are you doing back here?" I finally manage. "Just visiting?"

"Nope. It's permanent. We moved. My mom even got her old job back." Tanner looks straight at me as he says this. "Mom decided that once you live by the ocean, it ruins you for anywhere else forever, so we may as well give in and return, because why postpone the inevitable, you know?"

I smile at this. I can't help it. "You're here for good? Seriously?"

"Uh-huh." Tanner's eyes finally shift, scanning the beach, two spots of red dotting his cheeks.

Is he *blushing*? And now I am too. Gah, gah, gah! I need to end this conversation before it makes me any more crazy. Plus the sun tells me it's getting late and I need to be on my way to practice, which, at the moment, makes me feel relieved. "Hey," I blurt. "So unfortunately I've got places to go, and really soon."

"I'm sure," he says, and takes a step closer to me. His skin is already dark from the sun, and I remember how he was one of those blond boys who got tanned, not burned in the summer. "So when do we get to hang out and catch up for real? Got some time later today?"

"Um, no. I have practice."

"All day?"

"Yeah, actually," I say, shifting from one foot to the other, the sand rough and shifting under my feet. "Pretty much until I have to go home for dinner."

"After dinner, then?"

"I have to go to bed by ten. I need my rest."

"Wow. That's rough."

"Not really. It's just my life. I'm used to it."

"What about tomorrow?"

"I do the exact same thing tomorrow."

He shakes his head. "Wait, let me guess: This is your schedule every day this summer."

"Just about," I say, grabbing my towel, backpack, and flip-flops from the sand. "I'm training for Regionals."

"You don't have a single day off between now and then? A day when you don't go to practice or a competition?"

"Technically, we don't practice on Sundays," I say, "but I

usually go to the gym to work on my technique. The exciting life of a gymnast," I add with a roll of my eyes.

"So am I never going to get to catch up with you?"

"That would be nice," I say, as another bloom of red warms my cheeks. "But right now it's ten thirty-five, and if I don't leave, I'll be late for practice and have to face the wrath of my coach. I hope we run into each other again, though."

"Good to know," he says. "Me too."

I smile big this time. "See you soon, then," I say, and start on my way, my feet stepping and slipping toward the path that cuts through the dunes. The smile stays on my face all the way to the gym.

CHAPTER FIVE

We're all stars. Get it?

There is a word — no, a *name* — scrolling through my mind on repeat, and the repetition is making me kind of giddy.

Tanner, Tanner, Tanner.

My friend Tanner has moved back to town. And somehow he turned *gorgeous* between the last time I saw him on the playground and today. And he wants to see me again!

But I can't. Shouldn't.

Sigh.

This is no time for boy-obsessing, because practice is about to start, and practice is serious. Distractions lead to falls and injuries and the end of a gymnast's career. This is exactly why Coach has a No Boys Allowed policy. Boys are dangerous to a gymnast's concentration. It's true too.

Despite this, my mind goes right back to where it was before: *Tanner, Tanner, Tanner.*

"Why the dreamy smile, Joey?"

It takes a minute to register that someone is talking to me. I turn to see Trish leaning against the wall of the gym a few yards from the entrance, next to a mural of a leaping gymnast in a blue leotard. The toe of her front leg points straight at Trish, as if to say, *Live gymnast here!*

"Hey, Trish," I say, heading over to give her a quick hug. I'm suddenly envious of the way her long blond hair, gathered into a ponytail, falls in soft curls to the middle of her back. My dark hair seems so boring in comparison.

"So what were you thinking about, hmm?" she asks, her eyes curious but sweet.

I could tell Trish about Tanner and she wouldn't tell another soul, because her heart's so good that she's immune to even the juiciest gossip. But I worry that if I say something out loud to another living, breathing person, then the temptation to keep Tanner on my mind will only get worse. "Oh, I was just day-dreaming about sticking my beam routine."

She gives my arm a squeeze. "You can do it, Joey. You *will*. Next competition, it will happen. I'm sure of it."

"Thanks, Trish," I say.

She glances around the parking lot. "Where's Alex today?"

I shrug. "Not here yet, I guess. Maybe she's taping up her ankle — I'm sure it's hurting after yesterday."

"Do you think she's coming?"

"Of course. Just because you win gold doesn't mean Coach gives you a day off," I say with a laugh. The bloody rip at the center of my palm suddenly stings, a reminder of the pain I'll have to block out on bars today.

"I guess," Trish says. "I wouldn't know anything about winning gold, though."

"Your time will come too, Trish."

She smiles. "So are you going to wait out here for Alex?"

"Probably."

"I'll see you inside, then," she says, pushing off the wall and heading toward the entrance, her ponytail swinging from side to side with each step.

Now it's my turn to wait by the painted, pointed toe at the end of the gymnast's leg. Since I'm shorter than Trish, the gymnast's foot reaches toward my jaw, as if she wants to kick me in the head. After a minute, I check my phone for the time. 10:55 A.M. Where is Alex? An SUV turns into the lot, followed by an old gray pickup truck. One of the younger girls — Susie, I think — gives her mother a peck and opens the door of the SUV, blocking the truck from pulling into the only open spot left.

As it sits there idling, I notice Alex in the passenger side. Her mother drives a tiny silver Toyota and her father, a Jeep. I know this because I've been getting rides from Alex's family for as long as I can remember. Before I can check out the mystery driver, the SUV takes off and the truck swerves into the parking space. Through its dusty back window, I can just make out Alex's outline. It's weird that she's wearing her curly hair down this close to the start of practice. The person next to her is definitely not her mother, her father, nor even her older brother. But it's definitely a guy, and he's definitely young, though obviously not too young to drive. Alex and he are just sitting there, staring at each other, her profile edged with the sun's glow.

Is Alex with a *boy*? A boy she *likes*? Is today National Boys-Talk-to-Gymnasts Day or something? I can't believe she hasn't said anything to me.

Suddenly, I feel like I'm intruding on something private. But I can't make myself turn away either. If Alex has a real boyfriend, someone she hangs out with enough that he drives her around, she could get booted off the team if she isn't careful. And she's not being careful, letting him drop her off like this. What if *Coach* saw her? One time, he caught our former teammate (emphasis on *former*) Ashley November kissing a boy a few blocks away from the gym. Coach drove by and saw them. He gave her one chance to break it off, and when she didn't, bye-bye, Ashley. But Coach would never do that to his current Gansett Darling. Would he?

And what do *I* do? Wait here? Or leave Alex to her, um, whatever he is?

Better to go inside and pretend none of this happened, I decide, and I leave the painted gymnast without anyone to point to. My mind spins around the possibility of boys, boys, boys in our lives, and the way they've shown up so fast, when only moments ago, they didn't seem to exist at all.

The rush of air-conditioning after so much heat raises goose bumps on my arms. I hurry through the lobby to the changing area in the back, stripping off my T-shirt and stepping out of my shorts as I go, doing my best to ignore the sting of so many photographs of my sister along the way. Julia winning the gold medal at Regionals. Julia winning the gold medal at a local rivalry competition. Julia winning another gold medal at another Regionals, and of course, Julia up on that top podium when she won gold for the All-Around at Nationals, tears of joy streaming down her face.

There is a chorus of "Hi, Joey!'s" from some of the younger girls when I reach the cubbies. Everyone is putting away their things, and some of them are in front of the mirrors applying lipstick.

"Hi, guys," I say. I want to tell them that gymnasts do *not* wear makeup to practice, only at important competitions, and that putting on lipstick before practice is a sign that they are not and never will be serious medal contenders. Then I remember the way my head has been in the clouds about Tanner for the last half hour and wonder whether I should be doling out advice. Alex still hasn't come in, so I shove my T-shirt and shorts into my cubby on top of my flip-flops and head inside the gym to begin warming up without her.

Coach Angelo shakes his head when he sees me, meaning he's still disappointed about my fall from beam. I hate the first practice after a competition. It's always about paying for your sins of the day before.

Trish is stretching in the far corner of the floor and I make my way to her, stepping over my teammates like they are driftwood littered along the beach. "Where's Alex?" Trish whispers.

"I don't know," I lie, getting down into a straddle split. The clock on the wall reads 11:01 A.M. Alex is officially late. Coach will not be pleased, but he doesn't seem to have noticed yet. He's standing in front of the far wall, deep in conversation with our assistant coach, Maureen, right under the blue and white banner that says, AT GANSETT, WE ARE ALL STARS! in gigantic block letters. Without fail, those words make me roll my eyes. Scattered across the long cinder-block wall, above the runway for the vault, are more signs with your standard gymnastics wisdom. JUST STICK IT! is up there a number of times, along with FEAR IS

Not Allowed in this Gym! and Gymnastics Is My Life! The sign that reads No Pain, No Gain! is the biggest one, and has the place of pride right next to the main banner. Every time you land — or don't land — your vault, when you turn to go back up to start again, you have to face these words.

"Hey, Joey," says Heather Aronson, who's warming up a few feet away from Trish and me. "Too bad about that fall yesterday." Her eyes blink wide and innocent.

I count to ten in my head. "Yeah, thanks," I say calmly. Almost no one on our team likes Heather. She's constantly reminding everyone about what went wrong at competitions, lording it over us as though she's always perfect. Which she's not. But she has a nightmare of a mother who constantly criticizes her, no matter how well she does at a meet, and who's so invested in her daughter's gymnastics career that she even chooses her floor exercise music, which, most recently, is some sort of boring, tinkly opera piece. This doesn't excuse Heather's annoying qualities, but when I have to deal with her, it helps to remember how difficult her family is.

I'm done with my split stretches, so I bring both legs together, my toes pointed, and press my torso flat against my thighs, my body like a folded up jackknife. When I straighten up, I see Alex approaching. Her face is flushed, and I doubt it's just from the heat outside. She is smiling too, despite the fact that she is limping, and clearly oblivious to the stares from our teammates. Whether they're staring because Alex is late or because of yesterday's win or because, as always, she is the Gansett Stars Darling, I'm not sure.

Was my smile like that after I saw Tanner?

The mere thought makes me shudder. My job is to focus, train, and win, not swoon over some stupid boy.

Alex slides down into a split next to Trish and me. "Do you think Coach noticed I'm late?" she whispers.

Trish just shrugs.

I arch into a back bend, my arms pressed against my ears, straightening my legs to curve my body into a half-heart shape, and hold myself there, my eyes on Alex even though I am upside down. "Coach always notices," I tell her. "You know that."

Alex sighs, but the smile doesn't leave her face. "Sometimes I wish . . ."

"You wish what?" I ask before straightening up. I want Alex to pull me aside and confess everything, but she's staring into space as if I hadn't spoken at all. A minute goes by before I give up. "Listen, I'm warmed up already, so I'm going to head to beam before Coach yells at me to get over there."

Alex comes out of her daydream to give me an encouraging look. "Show him you can stick the layout, Joey. You can do it," she says, her tone fierce.

I smile back, grateful for her support, sure, but more relieved to see the Alex I know and love again. I get up and walk straight past the row of low practice beams that sit barely an inch off the ground, to the one high beam set out in front of all the other ones like a showpiece along one edge of the spring floor.

I hop up, walk to one end, and before I can become nervous or psych myself out or even remember my fall from yesterday, I stare down the ends of my fingertips, arms outstretched in a straight line just below eye level. I swing them up and over my head into a perfect back handspring, right into the highest, most confident back layout I've ever thrown on beam.

And I stick it.

"Woohoo! Go, Joey," cheer Alex and Trish. A few other teammates whistle their appreciation.

My arms rise up over my head in a flourish, posed and proud. When I turn to dismount, Coach Angelo is standing on the blue mat below, his arms crossed, clipboard pressed against the left side of his body. His face is expressionless. I freeze.

"Where do you think you're going?" he asks, his voice cold.

"Um, I just . . . I knew you'd want me to do my back layout first thing, so I thought I'd get on it before you needed to tell me to."

"Joey, what *exactly* did you fall on yesterday? Was it a back handspring back layout?"

I hesitate, the inside of my stomach doing flip-flops. "Well . . . no."

"Don't play games. You're wasting time. Answer me."

I take a deep breath. "It was a back handspring, back handspring into a back layout."

"So what made you think that doing a single back handspring into a back layout would cut it?"

I open my mouth and close it, then open it again. "Nothing, I just —"

He raises a hand to cut me off. "Before you come down from that beam, Joey Jordan, you are to stick twenty tumbling passes without a single bobble. Do you understand?"

I swallow. Nod.

"You want to win, don't you?"

"Yes, Coach," I say, then decide to go for broke. "But, well —" Angelo's glare halts my words. "But what?"

"Um, ah," I say, stumbling, yet still determined. "I was thinking that maybe I'd do better, um, if we changed my routines to reflect my strengths."

Coach meets this challenge with a cold silence. "Ms. Jordan," he says finally, his voice sharp with anger. "Twenty passes. Now. Your feet will not touch this floor until you are done." He gives me a long, hard look before turning and walking away, as if I'd said nothing at all. "Alex," he barks. "Come here!"

The only sound is Alex's hurrying feet. Everyone else has gone silent. I don't need to look to know that all my teammates are watching me, waiting to see how I react. Inside, I know that my instincts are right, that with changes to my routine, I'd have a real chance at winning. But here at this gym, Coach's orders are law, so there is nothing else to do but obey. I walk to the very end of the beam, my bare feet pressing against the rough, springy texture, my toes gripping the edge with each step, and once again, I am staring down the ends of my fingertips, my arms outstretched, ready to launch into my first of twenty back handspring, back handspring, back layout passes — that is, twenty if I stick every single one in a row. I could be here for the full six hours of practice if I can't pull myself together.

"Come on, Joey."

I hear Trish's whisper off to my side, giving me courage, and I raise my head high.

Then, once again, I throw my hands over my head to carry out the sentence Coach handed down, even if it takes me all day to do it.

CHAPTER SIX

The trouble with boys.

As I'm dressing to go home after practice, taking care not to touch the dark, purple bruises developing on the side of my right leg from my three-hour stint on the beam, Alex surprises me.

"So do you want to walk back to your house together and hang out a while? Maybe we can swim," she says.

I turn to her, eyebrows raised. I thought maybe Truck Boy would be picking her up too. "Definitely," I say, slipping my feet into my flip-flops. "I'm ready if you are."

But Alex is busy in front of the mirror, removing the elastic from her ponytail, fixing her hair. What has gotten into her? Does she think Truck Boy will be at the pool along with us or something? Everyone else disappears, saying their good-byes, until Alex and I are the only ones left.

Our assistant coach, Maureen, pokes her head through the door to the changing area. Her dark eyes light up with her smile.

"Great job, Joey," she says.

"Really?" I ask. Practice felt devoted entirely to my punishment on beam, which barely left time for even a few quick trips through my routines on the other events. Also, Maureen usually stays out of our path if Coach is on the rampage with one of us.

"Your form is impeccable on floor and beam too, but your grace and that flexibility . . ." She stops, as if searching for the right words. "It's breathtaking to watch. And I was thinking about what you said. . . ."

I look at her, confused. "What did I say?"

"On beam today. You were talking to Angelo about adjusting your routines to emphasize those strengths. I think we should try it."

I perk up. "We should?"

She smiles, but I can tell she's nervous. Nobody "adjusts" routines without the approval of Coach, and I highly doubt Maureen has gotten a green light from him. "Yes. Let me think about how for a bit and then I'll get back to you. All right?"

"Sure," I say, curious what she might have in mind, yet doubtful I'll ever have the chance to find out. Coach is unlikely to change his mind, especially since I dared suggest the idea first, and you don't go against him, not without dire risk to your place on the team. I can't help but be at least a little hopeful, though. It's nice to dream about things going my way. "Thanks. Maybe I'll spend some time thinking about how too."

"Good," she says, shutting the door and returning to the gym.

Alex finishes with her hair. Finally. "Well, *that* was interesting."

"Maybe Coach knows?"

"Right. Like you haven't been wanting to change your routines forever and he's forbidden it."

I think about Julia saying there's more than one way to impress the judges, that it doesn't always have to be about power and tumbling. "Maybe it's time I defy Coach for once. Prove to him that he's been wrong all along."

Alex's expression is so skeptical I might have just told her that the sun isn't coming up tomorrow or I met a real-life werewolf or that Sarah Walker is actually a nice person.

"You never know," I say. "He might come around."

"Don't get your hopes up, Joey," she says, grabbing her stuff and limping down the long hallway lined with Julia glory to the exit.

But the thing is, they already are.

Alex and I don't say anything else until we get outside, the heat greeting us with its sticky tongue, promising that the walk to my house will be gross.

"I can't wait to get in the pool," I say.

Alex smiles. She knows what's coming. "I know. Me too."

"Race you, then? Because why not make this trip even more disgusting and the water even better when we get there?"

"Of course," she says.

"Ready, set" — I give her a look and she nods — "go!"

Despite the humidity and the bruises marking our bodies and the fact that Alex is favoring one ankle, she and I take off running, out of the parking lot and past the Dairy Queen and Tony's Pizza, the T.G.I. Friday's and the other assorted chain restaurants, through the center of town and then down along the beach. We fly past the ocean, me in the lead, then Alex, then me again, both of us picking up speed, all thoughts of our hurts forgotten, our strides longer and longer as we turn away from the waves and the long stretch of sand toward my house, which is just a few streets away now. We arrive at my front lawn at the exact same moment, so it's a tie, and both of us lie down on the grass, our breaths coming in heaves, laughing.

"Like we really needed to go for a jog after practice," Alex says.

"I know. But it's kind of tradition, right?"

Alex smiles, propping herself up on her elbows. "It is."

"All right, I'm going swimming," I say, getting up and brushing away the blades of grass that are sticking to my skin. "Are you coming?"

"Yup," she says.

We traipse through the house, Alex calling out "Hey, Mrs. Jordan" toward my mother's studio before we head out the screen door onto the deck. Alex ducks into the bathhouse to change into her swimsuit and then it's my turn. We pile our discarded workout clothing in a heap on a chair, and soon Alex is stepping onto the diving board at one end with me right behind her.

"Any requests?" she wants to know, bouncing a little.

"How about a double back?"

"Done," she says, turning around to face me, positioning herself at the very edge of the springy board, standing high on her toes. She jumps once before taking off into two lightning-speed, perfect somersaults, and then splashes into the water.

"Come on, Joey," Alex calls out to me. "The temperature is perfect."

"So what'll it be?"

She looks thoughtful, bobbing in the deep end, her hair slicked back from her forehead, making her eyes seem even bigger than usual. "A full twist, I think?"

"You got it," I say, readying myself at the back of the board. I take two practiced strides, then launch myself from the end like I am heading into a vault, feeling that familiar freedom of being shot into the air. But instead of Coach's watchful, critical eye to worry about, there is only blue sky and sun and my body whipping around until my eyes spot the board's edge, and my toes and then the rest of me plunge through the pool's surface.

When I come up for air, I'm smiling. Swimming out here is perfect after a grueling practice. Alex has already claimed her favorite inner tube, and she's floating in the shallow end, her knees slung over one end, her back against the other. She paddles in my direction, dragging another water ring with her. I climb over the side and sink into the middle, keeping one hand on Alex's tube so we stay close together.

I already know what I want to say and I wonder if Alex can sense what's coming. "So . . ."

Alex twirls around so she faces me, circles swirling out from the inner tube toward mine. "So?"

"Before practice today . . ."

A guilty look crosses her face. "You saw me, didn't you?"

"Well, I don't know. Was there *actually* something to see?"

"I don't know. Maybe." Her voice has become small, but there is excitement underneath it, like she's dying to get this out.

And I, her dear friend, will help in this time of need. "Spill, Alex," I say, blocking the sun's glare with a hand over my eyes. "Who's the guy? And since when is there a guy? And since when is the guy driving you around? *In his truck?*"

"One question at a time, please." She grins.

My jaw drops. She is actually enjoying this. "Stop stalling!"

"You can't tell *anybody* or I'll be in so much trouble."

"Yeah, you would. Coach would kick you off the team for breaking the number one rule. And *no*, I'm not going to tell." I look at her with mock offense.

"I met him at the diner downtown one night last week — he's working there for the summer. I walked in to pick up our take-out and he was running the cash register and we got to talking and . . ." She trails off, like the rest is obvious.

"And . . . ?" I prompt Alex to finish.

"You know."

I flick water at her. "Um, no, actually, I don't. How you get from *hello* to a boy giving you a ride somewhere is a total mystery to me. But I'm *sure* you're going to give me all the details."

Alex splashes me back. "He asked my name and I asked his and he got my number and then he called."

"He called you!" Not once has a boy ever called the house asking for me. "When?"

"That same night. And every night since."

She drops this like it's nothing.

"Alex! You're just telling me this now? I can't believe you." This time I flip her out of the inner tube and crashing into the pool. She fully deserves it for holding back, and I don't feel an ounce of guilt.

When she comes up from under the water, she's too giddy to be angry. "I like him, Joey."

"Yeah, I can see that. You've got a gooey look on your face and you're not the slightest bit annoyed that I dunked you."

"Maybe a little," she says, but she is smiling wide.

I can't help but laugh at this. "What's his name?"

"Tommy. Tommy Ayers," she says, struggling to settle back onto the inner tube, her eyelashes glittering with beads of water. "He's sixteen and he's from the West Coast and he is totally, utterly dreamy." Alex rests her head against the float, staring up at the sky.

"I hate to be the bearer of reality, but —"

"Joey, don't say it," she cuts in before I can finish.

"Somebody has to, Alex. And if no one else knows, then I guess it's my job to do it."

"I don't want to hear it. I don't want to be reminded that I can't have a boyfriend, that gymnastics is more important than everything else, that we need to make sure our priorities are straight. I've heard it all before."

"Good. So then you know you have to stop seeing him before Coach finds out."

"I won't, though."

"But Alex —"

"Stop," she interrupts again.

"— I don't know what I'd do if Coach kicked you off the team!"

Alex puts a finger to her lips to shush me.

"Fine," I say, relenting, and for a while, we float in silence, the lapping of the water against the sides of the pool the only sound other than the occasional bird tweeting overhead. Alex drifts into the deep end while I stay in the shallows, one hand gripping the pool's edge, thinking. Eventually I call out, "So I guess I have some news too."

"Yeah?"

I nod.

She paddles toward me until she can grab my float and lock on to it. "Well, tell me already."

I take a deep breath. I know I need to get this out. Once it's in the open, I can move on. "I saw T.J. today."

Alex's eyes widen. "T. J. Hughes? From years ago?"

I can feel my cheeks redden. "Yes. Though he now goes by Tanner."

"And?"

"And nothing. I just ran into him down on the beach. End of story."

"Joey." Alex's tone is scolding. "I know you're holding back."

"I'm not."

"You are."

"What do you want to know that you think I haven't told you?"

"Is he cute or what?"

I close my eyes a moment and remember the way his hair curled down around his eyes and the sides of his face, the smile full of mischief, the big eyes, and the laughter in his voice. "I suppose so."

"Right. Uh-huh. So he was exceedingly adorable."

I give Alex a look. "It wouldn't matter if he was the hottest guy in the universe, because *we can't be thinking about boyfriends*. Now isn't the time. We can worry about dating boys after we retire. Then we'll have plenty of time for romance."

"Okay, Coach Angelo."

"Hey! It's just the truth. It's what we signed up for when we decided we wanted to compete at Nationals one day. And, ideally, the Olympics."

Alex's expression turns serious. "I'm not so sure anymore, Joey. My ankle has been hurting me for over a year and I'm tired of all this pain."

Goose bumps ripple across my forearms. I'm suddenly afraid of what Alex might say next, where this is going. "You're not sure about *what*?"

"I'm not sure I agree that boys are for later, and I'm not sure I want Nationals anymore, and I'm not sure the sacrifices are worth it."

"But, Alex, you're the best on our team! You always win! If anyone has a shot at winning the gold at Regionals in August, it's *you*! You would give all of that up? How could you?"

"Easy," Alex says, popping up out of the inner tube with a loud splash and planting her feet in the shallow end. "I would just quit."

Before I can recover from the shock, before I can say another word in protest, Alex is out of the pool and heading toward the bathhouse to change. She wraps a towel around her hair so it covers her ears, like she's already telling me she can't hear me.

Set daily, monthly, and long-term goals and dreams.

Don't ever be afraid to dream too big.

Nothing is impossible.

If you believe in yourself, you can achieve it.

— NASTIA LIUKIN, USA,

2008 Olympic All-Around champion

CHAPTER SEVEN

Fireworks everywhere.

A few days pass, and by the Fourth of July, everything goes back to normal. Well, everything goes back to the *appearance* of normal, but I know better. Things are changing. I can't stop thinking about Tanner and wishing I'd run into him, and I can't stop thinking about Maureen's promise to help me figure out new routines either. Alex has lost some of her luster at the gym, but out in the world, she glows. The reverse used to be true. I don't know what to make of it.

"Alex, Alex!" Coach shouts at practice, heading toward us. We've just rotated from vault to bars, and I'm warming up on one set while Alex warms up on the other. She drops down from the high bar. "Your form is atrocious. Your back isn't straight, your legs are like jelly. What is going on with you?"

Alex just shrugs, like she doesn't care. "Bad day, I guess," she says.

Coach stops at the edge of the floor and stares at her. "Champions can't afford bad days."

She's at the chalk box, her hands sending up thin clouds of white into the air. "I guess I'm not a champion, then," she mutters.

My jaw drops. Nobody talks back to Coach.

"What did you say?" he bellows.

She takes a deep breath. Plasters a smile on her face. "Nothing. Just that next time, I'll be more careful about my form."

"You're right, you will," Coach says, watching Alex for a long time before he turns to me. "Joey, you're up. Show me what you got."

I give Alex a guilty look over the chalk box. "Yes, Coach," I say.

"I don't care. Really," she whispers.

But I don't believe her.

When I'm chalked up and ready to go, I approach the low bar, eye level to it. The chatter of my teammates falls away and so do all the worries about Alex. I take one step across the mat, and another, then I launch into a kip, my hands on the bar, my body gliding smoothly underneath until I shoot up over it, hips along the curve, straight into a back hip circle. The momentum shoots me into a handstand, followed by another kip, but this time, it leads to a release move, and the high bar is just within reach. My hands grab it, sending up two puffs of chalk on impact, my palm screaming in protest even under the protection of the leather grips I wear. When my feet circle all the way to the top, my toes pointing straight at the ceiling, I hover there a moment before swinging into a series of giants, one after the other, my body extended and whipping around the high bar. Each one gets faster, more exhilarating, even while the friction on my hands becomes more and more intense, the velocity making me fly until, at just the right moment, I release the bar into a double back dismount. My feet come down straight and solid, and once I secure my balance, I throw my arms behind my ears, my back a slight, graceful arch.

The smile on my face is huge. I can't wipe it away. Nailing a routine like that is one of the things I love most about gymnastics.

"What's gotten into you, Joey?" Coach asks, but his voice isn't unkind — he sounds impressed. "That was the best bar routine I've seen from you yet."

I drop my hands to my sides and turn to him, still smiling. I don't know what's gotten into me either, but whatever it is — the additional conditioning, the hope of gold at Regionals — I'll take it. "Thanks, Coach," I say.

Angelo shakes his head. "It's like you and Alex switched bodies."

My smile falls away, and I can't look at Alex, that guilty feeling from before planting itself in my middle once again. Coach can be so mean, even when he's trying to say something nice. Then I hear a door slam, the one by the changing area. When I turn toward the sound, Alex is gone.

The clock says 5:55. At least practice is almost over. I wonder whether she'll wait for me like she's supposed to, or take off down to the beach for the Fourth of July celebration without me. To be honest, I can't decide which one I'd prefer. We've never dealt with this before — me exceeding Alex at practice. Alex has always been the star.

Before I can think too much more about this, Maureen waves me over.

"How are you doing, Joey?" she asks, sounding concerned.

"I'm okay, Coach."

She searches my face. "Are you really?"

"Of course," I say, but I can tell she doesn't believe me. She knows Alex and I are best friends and that I'm worried about her.

"You need to focus on you, Joey. You're only responsible for you when you're in this gym."

If only that were true. But her comment reminds me of something that's been on my mind almost constantly these last few days. "Maureen, I've been thinking about what you said." My voice is a whisper. I don't want Coach Angelo to hear. "About making some changes to my floor and beam routines."

Maureen's eyebrows arch. She looks interested. "And?"

I take a deep breath. "And . . . if you're willing to help, I'm in."

A smile appears on her face, as if she has a secret. "Can you meet me here on Friday night at nine P.M.?"

Now it's my turn to smile. We *are* keeping secrets. I'm surprised how satisfying it feels to defy Coach Angelo, even a little. "Is it okay if Julia brings me?"

"Yes, I think that would be fine," she says. "So you'll make the arrangements?"

I nod. Maureen turns, but before she can go, I reach out and stop her.

"Thank you," I say. "For being willing to do this."

She gives me a serious look. "Ultimately, Joey, this isn't about me. It's all up to you," she says, and walks away, calling out to the girls on the low beams, "Chin up, Avery! Poise, Tanya!" as she goes.

And intimidating as this is, I know it's the truth.

Alex *does* wait for me. But our walk down to the ocean is silent. Awkward. Tense. I want to fix things, but I don't know how. I've always done my best to fight the feelings of jealousy I have sometimes about Alex when it comes to gymnastics, so I can't help wondering now if Alex is jealous of me for once, and how I performed today at practice.

"Hey, girls," my mother says when we find her on the beach. She's sitting with Mrs. Tamsen, Alex's mom, on a series of blankets spread across the sand. Before they noticed us, they were deep in conversation, and Mrs. Tamsen has a guilty look on her face as she turns our way. I bet they were talking about Alex and me.

"Hi, Mom," I say and point to her cheek. "You have a spot of blue on the side of your face."

"Oh well. I'll get it later."

I resist the urge to roll my eyes at my ultrastereotypical-artist mother. On top of the paint splotch, she's dressed like a hippie, with a long flowing tank dress covered in flowers. "Hi, Mrs. Tamsen," I say to Alex's mom.

She smiles. "Nice to see you, Joey."

Alex doesn't say a word to her mother or mine, just drops her gym bag onto one of the towels and kicks off her flip-flops. "I'm going to the bathroom to change," she says to no one in particular and heads toward the pavilion.

Mom raises her eyebrows. "Rough practice?"

"Not for me," I say, leaving my flip-flops next to Alex's and stripping off my tank top and shorts. Unlike Alex, I changed into my swimsuit before I left the gym.

The beach is already packed with people celebrating the Fourth, getting ready for tonight's fireworks and whatever else kids who actually have social lives do. Gymnasts, well, we hang out with our families and other gymnasts, because those are the only people we have time for in our lives. So Alex and I sitting with our mothers at the beach is not unusual. It's just what we've always done.

My eyes search the beach to see if Trish's family is here yet. Instead, I spy Julia and Madison playing volleyball a ways off with a bunch of guys and girls who must be in college too. College students always have this look about them, you know? You can just tell they're no longer in high school from their confidence. A few blankets over from us, I pick out Mrs. Walker, Sarah Walker's mother, which means Jennifer Adams's family must be somewhere nearby as well.

I really don't feel like engaging in gym rivalry drama tonight. It's bad enough that Alex is acting so weirdly.

Speaking of Alex, she's making her way back from the pavilion.

And she's wearing a bikini.

Red, with little white polka dots all over it.

My old, faded black tank suit suddenly feels ugly and immature. Like it's more appropriate for someone far younger than a girl who will turn fourteen this fall. I look down my flat board of a body and notice the frayed edges of the nylon material. It may as well be another practice leotard that I wear at the gym, it's so unflattering, especially now that Alex looks so sparkly in her new two-piece.

"So what do you think?" she asks, tugging at the thin red strap that's tied in a bow around the back of her neck. Her long hair flows in soft curls around her shoulders.

"Depends how you mean," I say.

She sighs. "Joey, just say it."

"Technically, you look amazing. I mean, most girls would kill for your body."

"But . . . ?"

"But *what's* gotten into you lately?" I notice our mothers have stopped talking in order to hear what Alex and I are saying. I yank her farther down the beach and lower my voice. "Since when do you prance around the beach wearing a bikini?"

Alex's face colors.

Ugh. I am being a judgmental jerk, I sound like her mother, *and* I've embarrassed her. Awesome. "I'm sorry," I say. "I'm not being supportive, am I?"

She shakes her head and turns away.

"You're right. And if I showed up dressed like that, I would want you to tell me I look amazing and leave it there."

Alex's eyes land on me again and she is glaring. "Dressed like *what*?"

Oops. "I can't say anything right at the moment, can I?"

She shrugs, searching the sand, shoving some of it around with her left big toe. "I should've told you I bought it and that I planned to wear it tonight. I don't know why I've been holding things back lately. I just, I don't know — some things feel so new and different I don't even know how to talk about them. So I don't say anything at all, I guess."

"Alex, I'm sorry. I know you have a lot on your mind" — *like potentially quitting the sport that involves everything you've ever dreamed of your entire life* — "and I want to be a good best friend, not a pain. Sometimes I don't know how to talk about this stuff either."

She looks at me again. She's coming around, I can tell.

"Forgive me?"

She smiles a bit sheepishly. "There's nothing to forgive, so yeah, of course."

"The bathing suit is adorable, by the way. Though I couldn't get away with wearing it."

"Why not?" she asks, frowning.

"Because my parents would never let me hear the end of it. They'd take it as a sign that I'm" — and I put on my best imitation Mom face, conjuring my version of her tone of voice — "*finally developing into a young woman*, which is code for Joey is ready to retire from gymnastics and have a normal life. At least that's how my dad would put it."

"All that from a bikini?"

"I know. Seems crazy, right? But that's the way the Jordan parentals roll."

Alex laughs. Things are getting back to normal. Hoo-ray. I decide to go for broke.

"So," I say. "How's the ankle feeling?"

Alex eyes me. "Better. Much. Why?"

"Well, shall we try the back handsprings today or the hand walking?"

A smile grows on Alex's face as she pretends to ponder the difficulty of this question. This makes me happy. Some things *do* stay the same. Some people play volleyball at the beach, some people just sit around in the sun, some people go running. And gymnasts, well, we do gymnastics.

"I think back handsprings, since it's the Fourth," she decides.

I give her a mock quizzical look. "Why are handsprings better for the Fourth?"

"Oh, I don't know. They're flashier, I think."

"A double back would be flashier."

"Yes, but not as fun to do in the sand, and you can't get as far down the beach with double backs. You do one and then it's over."

"True." Then I realize there's a potential wrench in our fun as I take in Alex's choice of swimsuit. "Um, I hope you tied that top on tight," I say.

"Oh. Right." She walks back toward the beach blankets where our mothers are trying not to stare at us, but doing a terrible job at hiding their interest. She scoops up a T-shirt, pulls it over her head, and tucks the ends underneath the edge of her bikini bottom so it doesn't ride up, the same way we sometimes do with our leotards when we are at practice. This cracks me up.

"What do you think?" she asks, giving a turn.

"I think it works."

"Let's go, then," I say, and we take off jogging toward the water where the tide has gone out, leaving behind the firm sand that's perfect for doing gymnastics.

"Do you think you can make it past that lifeguard chair this time?" Alex points down the beach toward an old wooden perch with the number 3 painted on a sign attached to the side. A girl in a bright orange swimsuit sits at the top, her eyes on the people swimming in the surf.

We've been flipping for almost an hour, long enough for the sun to have begun its descent toward the horizon. It's amazing how doing gymnastics at the beach can feel so different from doing it at practice, how the fun of it can make us forget everything that happens at the gym.

"I don't know. Can you make it?" I ask her.

"Sure. Why not? Let's see who gets there first."

I laugh. "You're *really* going to challenge me with back handsprings?"

Alex smiles. "I guess so. Looks like we have a clear path too. But we won't for long, so come on."

"Fine, fine," I say, turning to her. "Ready?"

She nods.

"Set . . . go!"

Both of us run down the shoreline into a round-off back handspring. When our feet land, we immediately stretch into another and then another, each one covering more ground than the last as our momentum picks up. Flip-flops are one of the most basic moves a gymnast can master, but that doesn't change the fact that they are fun. Your body showing off how powerful it can be, the way your hands whip over your head, coupled with the perfect arch in your back and the force of your legs driving toward the ground — it's exhilarating.

As I pound across the beach, my hands and feet kick up tufts of sand, packed hard from the crush of the waves earlier in the day before the tide went out. The sound of the surf sizzling as it rushes toward the shore makes me excited for a swim. This tumbling run is it for me today, I decide, and probably for Alex too, but our plan to reach the lifeguard chair is cut short by two trolls.

Sarah Walker and Jennifer Adams stand there facing us, their hands on their hips.

"Aren't you two the adorable pair," Sarah says.

"The Gansett Darling Duo," Jennifer says with a smirk. "Is that what you're called?"

Alex glares at them. "Well, I thought it was pretty sweet the way you two wept for me the other day."

Jennifer looks confused. "What are you talking about?" she asks.

"Oh, you know. When I won the gold medal for All-Around, and you were so happy for me you cried?"

"It won't always be you up there," Sarah hisses.

"Yeah. Maybe next time, it will be Joey," Alex says, grabbing my arm. "Come on, we're going for a swim. See you later, ladies!"

We walk toward the water and a wave thins out across our feet. The temperature is cool but refreshing after so many hours working out.

"Thanks for standing up to them," I say to Alex as the surf rises to our knees. Kids are splashing in the water around us. A bunch of guys plays keep-away to our left. "I'm always speechless around those two. Especially Sarah."

"No problem. At least some things don't change."

"What do you mean?"

"Sarah and Jennifer may be able to dish it out, but I can dish it right back. You need to learn to do it too, Joey."

"Not really," I say, giving her a playful shove, wading farther in. "I'll always have you for that."

Before Alex can respond, a huge wave rises in front of us, the top edged with white, getting higher and higher as though it's hesitant to crash. Alex and I both dive under it.

I come up first, breaking through the surface just as a baseball whizzes by my head. It makes a loud *plop* as it lands. The keep-away guys shout "Sorry!" as I bounce through the chest-deep water to retrieve it.

But someone else gets there first, swimming fast under the water, a hand closing around the ball as he emerges from below. Water streams off him in torrents as he shakes off the excess, hair slicked back, his eyes fixed on me.

"Joey Jordan," he says with a grin. "We meet again."

"Hi, Tanner," I say, trying to minimize the giant smile that wants to cross my face.

"I knew that was you flipping down the beach."

Alex arrives and the three of us bob up and down in the waves.

"I don't know if you remember me, but I'm Alex," she says.

"Nice to meet you again."

"I heard you were back in town," she says. "From Joey."

His grin gets bigger. "So you've been talking about me," he says in my direction.

Before I can think of a comeback, one of the guys from the game calls out, "Hey, Hughes, any day now!"

"Gotta go. See you around," he says, and dives under the water, swimming away. We wait until we see him pop up and throw the ball back to the other guys.

It's Alex's turn to give me a shove. "He got *hot*, Joey."

"Did he? Hmm. I guess I didn't notice."

"Yeah, right, you didn't," she says.

I can tell she's about to try to dunk me, so I jump away, laughing and ducking under the water myself. The two of us stay in the ocean until our fingertips are wrinkled and the sky is a deep pink. With arms wrapped around our middles, shivering, we run up the beach to grab towels and dry off before the fireworks start.

Mrs. Hughes, Tanner's mother, is standing there chatting with my mom and Mrs. Tamsen. Her hair is thick and long and blond like her son's. She looks younger than most of the mothers I know, even mine.

"Joey!" Mom says the second I'm within earshot. "I can't believe you didn't mention that the Hugheses were back in town. Mary was just telling me that you ran into Tanner here last week."

I wipe my face with the towel, as much to hide as to dry off. When I pull it away and wrap it around my body, I see Mrs. Hughes wears a sympathetic expression. She clearly didn't mean to rat me out. "Hi, Mrs. Hughes," I say. "Welcome back."

"Thank you, Joey." She turns back to my mom. "I should have come by sooner anyway. It's been so busy at work. We got here and I hit the ground running. . . ." The three mothers huddle up again, continuing their conversation as though Alex and I aren't there.

Which is fine with me.

Alex and I do our best to soak up the water from our hair and head to the pavilion to change out of our wet bathing suits into shorts and T-shirts. By the time we return, it's almost dark, stars beginning to twinkle above us, a sliver of moon like a bright white cutout amid all that deep blue. The night is clear and warm. Perfect for fireworks.

When we're almost back to the blanket, Alex starts giggling.

"What?" I ask, suspicious.

She points and I follow the line of her finger.

Tanner Hughes is standing next to his mother, who is still chatting away with mine and Alex's. He looks incredibly awkward.

Okay, I'll be honest: incredibly awkward and really, *really* hot.

He shrugs when our eyes meet. "Hey," he says.

"Why don't you kids go find a good spot to watch the show?" my mother says. "That way you can catch up."

Alex answers for me. "Sure," she says, and then to Tanner, she asks, "Where should we go?"

My mouth opens again, but Tanner gets there first. "My friends and I are meeting up at lifeguard chair number four to see if we can claim it."

"That's a great idea," Alex says. "Right, Joey?"

"Um, yes, I suppose?" My tone goes up at the end like I've just asked a question, but I think I'm already agreeing to this plan.

Alex and Tanner are a ways down the beach before I pull myself together enough to run and catch up. On my way, I say a prayer to the goddesses of gymnastics — Nadia, Dominique, Nastia, and Ecaterina — asking them for the willpower to resist the temptation that is Tanner Hughes ahead of me, to stop noticing things like the way his blond hair curls at the nape of his neck, how his skin is tanned to a perfect golden color, and the muscles in his legs define themselves with each step. Gah! Perhaps I'm praying for blindness? Blindness feels like the only answer at the moment.

Alex, Tanner, and I don't say much until we near the lifeguard chair, when Tanner introduces us to his friends, who are hanging around drinking sodas and goofing off. One of the guys and Tanner exchange what could only be called a *meaningful look*, and my entire body flushes. Has Tanner been talking about me to his friends?

Uh-oh. I look up at the stars, as if my gymnastics goddesses might be hovering above, waiting for me to pray to them again.

"Joey . . . Joey?"

Alex nudges me. "Tanner is talking to you," she whispers.

I snap out of my little fantasy world. "Um, sorry. What?"

"You want to get up on the chair?" Tanner asks. "It'll have the best view of the fireworks."

"Uh, sure," I agree. Then to Alex, I say, "You're coming too," and grab her arm with one hand, using the other to climb the ladder along the side of the chair. At the top, I take a seat at the far right edge. When Alex tries to sit at the other end, leaving room for Tanner in the middle, I shake my head *no* and pat the spot next to me.

"Seriously, Joey?"

"Yes, seriously, Alex," I whisper.

She sighs and sinks onto the bench. Clearly, Alex thinks I am useless and confused when it comes to the species called boy.

And I fully admit: She is correct.

Tanner takes the only remaining place on the bench, to Alex's left. We sit there a while, the three of us, Alex talking to me, and Tanner leaning down to joke around with the guys hanging out below. But thanks to the excitement in the air at the beach, the sound of the waves crashing along the shore, and the warm breeze running across our skin, the initial awkwardness dissipates and I start having fun.

Eventually, Alex turns to me, and her face says that she's about to ask a favor.

"What, Alex?"

"Um, so . . . is it okay if I take off?" she blurts. "I kind of want to find Tommy." Alex's cheeks are flushed and her eyes shining just from saying this boy's name.

"Sure," I say. "Why not?" Who am I to stand in the way of love? Besides, she's been there for me all night. Time to reciprocate the favor.

"You really don't mind?"

"No. Not tonight I don't."

"Thanks, Joey," she says, giving me a quick hug. "Bye, Tanner," she adds before jumping down from our perch on the lifeguard chair and running off, leaving Tanner and me alone with only a narrow gap between us. Neither one of us moves even an inch.

Then Tanner turns to me. "I'm glad you were wrong," he says.

"What are you talking about?" I ask. "Wrong about what?"

"Well, you told me that the only thing you do all summer is practice at the gym. Clearly not, since here you are. And here we are, finally hanging out."

"But the Fourth of July is an exception," I say. "And I *did* tell you that eventually we'd find time to catch up. So I guess this is it."

Tanner gives me a look, his eyes alight with laughter. "Hmmm."

"What now?" I ask, trying not to smile, and grateful that it's gotten dark enough that he can't tell my cheeks are burning red.

"If there's at least one exception, I'm betting there are others too."

"Nope," I say with confidence. "Fourth of July is it. Then it's all train, train, train until Regionals in August."

"You're really devoted to gymnastics, huh?"

I lean my head back against the edge of the lifeguard chair. "I am. I have to be. I want to win gold. That's all I've ever wanted."

For a moment, Tanner is silent. Then he says, "You know, I get that. I feel that way sometimes about soccer, that I don't just want to be good, I want to be extraordinary. The kind of guy that leads the team."

"Yeah?" I ask, turning to him again, interested to hear this.

He nods. "The kind of guy who is as dedicated to soccer as you are to gymnastics."

This elicits a little smile. Tanner just complimented me — I think. Afterward we just sit there, staring at each other. I don't know for how long, but it feels like forever and an instant at once.

Tanner takes a breath, about to say something else, when the first fireworks whistle up into the air. Our eyes automatically shift skyward to watch them burst into streams of sparkling blues and whites and reds. In the rush of the light and the crackle of the gunpowder, I take in Tanner's profile, the way his hair curls along his forehead, the expression on his face, laughing and happy. For these few minutes, I let myself enjoy this, this moment when I might be like any other girl hanging out with a cute boy on the Fourth of July.

That's me tonight, I decide: Joey Jordan, just an ordinary girl.

CHAPTER EIGHT

Tons of personality.

On Friday, I search the house for Julia and find her swimming out back. The sun has almost set and the sky is ringed with pink, red, and orange. All week, I've been trying to get up the courage to tell her what I'm doing, my plan — with Maureen's help — to change my routines without Coach's blessing. I've decided it's worth it if it means I win gold. I know it is. "Hey," I say to her.

"Hey yourself," she says back.

"I have a favor to ask. You can't tell anybody about it, though."

Julia propels herself up and out of the pool, turning to sit along the edge, her legs still dangling in the water. "Ooh, a secret. I love secrets. Is it about a boy?"

I roll my eyes. "What is it with everybody's obsession with boys lately?"

She laughs, the sound like bells. "I don't know, Joey. You tell me. Who is obsessed with boys?"

"Nobody. Forget I said anything about them. The favor is something else entirely."

"Okay. Shoot."

"I need you to take me to the gym tonight."

"*That's* the secret? You have practice?"

"Not exactly."

Julia perks up again. "Then why?"

"Maureen is going to help me, ah, alter my floor and beam routines a bit."

"Does Angelo know?" She sounds interested.

"No. That's why it's a secret."

Julia stands up, water streaming from her bathing suit and legs onto the patio, then grabs a towel and begins to dry off. "If it's a favor for Coach, I'm in." Julia still thinks of Maureen as her coach, not Angelo.

"So you'll drive me?"

"I will. Be ready in fifteen minutes," she says, and heads inside to change.

"It's a favor for me too," I say softly, but she is already gone.

The parking lot at the gym is empty except for one other car — Maureen's, I assume. Julia pulls the key from the ignition and the engine quiets. I'm about to get out, but before I can, my sister turns to me.

"How are you feeling about gymnastics lately?"

It's so silent that it sounds like Julia is shouting. Or maybe it seems this loud because I hate getting this kind of Big Assessment Question about my commitment to the sport from members of my family. "Why is everyone so obsessed with the possibility of my quitting this summer?" I say. "Other people might be thinking of quitting, but I'm *not*."

Julia gives me a look. "Calm down, Joey. It was just a simple question."

I huff and puff in the passenger seat for a few seconds. Simple it isn't.

Julia waits. When she decides I'm done freaking out, she goes on, "I wasn't insinuating that you should quit. I only wanted to check in on how you're doing. You were really upset after the last meet, and now we're at the gym at night, when no one else is here, keeping secrets."

"Maureen's here."

"Obviously. But Angelo isn't."

"Just a few minutes ago you were intrigued about defying Angelo, and now suddenly you're not? This doesn't have to be a *we*, you know. Just a *me*. You're free to go. If you want," I add quickly.

"Would you like me to leave?"

I shrug. "It's up to you."

Julia sighs and looks at me in that *I'm your older sister and I'm just trying to protect you* way I've gotten used to after a lifetime of living with her. "I only want to make sure that you know what you are doing — what you're getting yourself into. Angelo could kick you off the team if you're going behind his back."

"I know. But I'm still going inside."

"Why don't I stay for a while, then? Until you see what's going on?"

"Fine," I sigh, like this is a burden, when really I kind of want Julia to stay. I complain a lot about getting compared to my older sister, the eternal Darling of the Gansett Stars, but somewhere deep inside, in a place I would never admit to having out loud, I occasionally let myself hope that Julia's magic will rub off on me. That if I hang around her long enough at the gym, or if she hangs around me, then I'll find out that Julia isn't the only one with a special destiny, and it's simply in the Jordan genes to win gold.

"Are you coming or what?" Julia says. "You don't want to be late for Maureen."

"All right, all right," I say, and we get out of the car.

Inside the gym, music is playing on the stereo.

Poppy, upbeat music. Not classical. Beethoven, Chopin, Mozart, movie soundtracks — that's the kind of music that's usually in the air when I'm here, because almost everyone uses classical music for their floor exercise routines these days. But this is different — the kind of music you want to dance around to in your bedroom when nobody is watching. The kind you sing along to in the car when it comes on the radio. Music you would actually download from iTunes because you like it. Just without the words.

Maureen watches for my reaction. She turns down the volume. "What do you think?"

"It's yours, isn't it?" Julia asks from over my shoulder. I thought she was going to stay in the lobby, out of sight, but suddenly it's the three of us. "The music from your floor routine back when you were a gymnast."

"Really?" I ask. "But this music is so unlike what we use today. It's . . . it's . . . so *fun*, it's so, I don't know, *danceable*, it's got tons of . . . of . . ."

"Tons of personality," Julia finishes for me. "That's what the sports commentators said about it."

"Yeah, that."

"About *you*," Julia adds, looking at Maureen.

Maureen smiles. "I'm glad you like it."

"Why?" I ask.

"Because it's about to become yours."

Julia throws her head back, laughing. Claps her hands with glee. "No way!" she exclaims. "That's fantastic."

"But only if you want it, Joey," Maureen adds.

"Coach *hates* this kind of music," I say.

"Yes, he does."

"He would *never* let me do my floor to that, no matter how much I liked it."

"Probably not, no," Maureen agrees. She walks up to me, puts her hands on my shoulders, and looks me in the eyes. I can hear Julia breathing behind me. "We are taking matters into our own hands."

"I know," I say, looking straight back at her to show that I am aware of the potential repercussions. "If Coach Angelo finds out, he'll be . . . beyond angry." I stop short of suggesting homicidal rage.

"Maybe."

I nod. "Oh yes."

"Is risking his fury worth it?" she asks.

I nod again, but more slowly this time. I'm excited and scared all at once. I want to do this so badly, but it's also something that could get me kicked off the team. Probably worse than dating a boy. "It is," I say finally. My turn to smile. "That music? I want it."

"Good. Because like this music, you, my dear, have tons of personality. You have grace, style, charm, and a whole lot more. It's a shame to let all that go to waste with the routine you do now. This is precisely what you need to win at Regionals this year. And just wait till you see what I have in store for your beam routine!"

With that, Maureen heads back toward the stereo, with Julia bouncing along behind her. My sister turns around twice to give me huge smiles and two thumbs-up, but I just stand there, unable to move, telling myself over and over that it's all going to be okay.

Over an hour later, Maureen has taken me step-by-step through my new floor routine, with Julia calling out pointers now and then. The more I go through this routine, the more excited I am. The initial upbeat go-around of the floor emphasizes my poise, grace, and dance abilities as it leads into the first tumbling pass, and then comes the second, complete with hand flourishes, leaps, and jumps. Then the perfect ending: a Shushunova straddle jump that turns into a full twist that drops me to the floor just before the final pose. It's fun, it's upbeat, it's unique, but most of all, it feels like it was made especially for me.

"So this was yours once?" I ask Maureen.

"More or less," she says. "I've revamped it a bit to fit your strengths."

"Really?"

"I've been thinking about using my old routine for a while."
She smiles. "I just needed the right gymnast to come along."

"The choreography is amazing."

Maureen's cheeks turn slightly red at the compliment. "I hoped you'd think that."

"I love it," I say.

"All righty, then. Let's do it again. From the top. Then we'll do an initial run-through on beam."

"Go, Joey!" my sister calls out from her perch on the vault, and I walk to the center of the floor and pose, ready to begin.

"You *really* think Coach Angelo won't notice what I'm doing?" I ask Maureen after three more run-throughs on floor and some time trying out some new moves on beam. We are on our way out the door to go home.

Maureen raises her eyebrows, her hand hovering over the light switch by the wall. "What does he pay attention to, Joey? Think hard before you answer."

Even in the shadows of the gym at night, the vault seems to stare me down. Then the uneven parallel bars. The beam. The floor exercise. I picture Coach Angelo here, at practice, barking orders and yelling about this and that. Height. Form. Technique. Momentum. Never, ever the dance moves on floor. Or the artistry between the truly quantifiable skills on beam. To Coach Angelo, these are all just filler between the real stuff. The stuff that counts. The stuff that the judges care about most. At least according to him.

"Coach Angelo watches the layouts and full twists and double backs. Tumbling passes. Vaults. And bar routines."

Maureen nods. Smiles.

"But he stops paying attention during the other parts of routines. Like he doesn't even notice they're happening."

"Exactly."

"Okay. *Maybe* I could get away with practicing a few skills on beam without Coach getting a clue for a while, especially if I try them on the beam in back, against the wall. But do you really think Coach isn't going to notice it if I suddenly have different music for floor? There's no way. He'd go into conniptions." I don't really know what a conniption is, but my mother is always accusing my father of having one, so I am certain that, at the very least, it's not a good thing.

"I agree. The new floor routine, the new music, that part is more complicated."

All the air flows out of my lungs upon hearing this, a long sigh of relief. Maureen doesn't expect me to take supercrazy risks, then, only mildly crazy ones.

"That's why you'll practice your new routine only at night, with me," Maureen goes on. "Every Friday until Regionals, we're going to work until it's perfect. And it *will* be perfect, Joey. You've got it in you. I *know* you do."

As much as I can't help but feel pride at Maureen's confidence in me, the kind of affirmation I've always longed to hear from Coach Angelo, I'm still concerned that I will get in trouble. That it will never work out the way we want, or worse, that I'll lose my spot on the Gansett Stars forever. But then my sister speaks up. "Joey, I think you should trust Maureen's gut. She knows what she's doing. Of all people, I know this is true."

I turn to Julia. "You think so?"

Julia looks at me, really stares at me, hard, intense, so I know she's serious. My sister has this way of making you believe that whatever she says will become real somehow. "Yes. And don't forget, this was your idea too."

I breathe deep. "I know."

"Don't worry yourself into the ground over it. Be happy. You were fantastic tonight," Julia drops, as though she compliments me like this all the time.

She doesn't. "Really? You think so?"

"Yes, Joey. I'm in if you are," she adds.

Maureen approaches the two of us and puts one hand on my back, the other on Julia's, so that the three of us are in a sort of huddle. It's like we're making a pact in the bluish glow of the darkened gym, and I start to feel the magic. I do. It is flowing from Julia and Maureen and swirling into the air around me, settling onto my skin, my bones, like fairy dust. And then Julia says the words that seal the deal, that make me believe that anything is possible.

"Sis, this is going to be your gold medal summer," she says. "I can feel it."

"Me too," I whisper, because I can.

Then the three of us walk out into the night.

There will be mistakes, there will be falters.

There will be things that are not a part of your plan.

See the challenges in your life and accept them and embrace them.

— DOMINIQUE DAWES, USA,

1996 Olympic gold medalist

CHAPTER NINE

Keeping secrets.

"You're awfully smiley lately," my father says when I enter the house one afternoon following practice. He is sitting in an easy chair in the living room — *his* chair — with his legs stretched out, his feet resting on an ottoman, a book across his lap. He wears an outfit that would embarrass the entire family if we were in public.

"Nah," I answer him, sinking down into the couch.

But my dad is right: I am smiley. I smile when I wake up in the morning, and when I go down to the beach to do drills and circuit training, and when I eat dinner at night, even if it's fish, and when I read *International Gymnast* before bed. I smile at practice too. For the first time in my life, maybe since the moment I walked into the gym as a second grader and felt what it was to fly, I believe I can do anything, that anything is possible. The fact that Maureen and my sister are taking all of this time out to train me and nobody else, that Maureen gave me her old floor routine and music and I'm doing well with all of it — it's having an effect on me. In the last couple of weeks, I've found that when I work to my strengths, everything else improves too.

"No, *really*, Joey," Dad insists. "You've had a smile on your face nonstop for the last two weeks. Ever since the fireworks." He puts his book on the side table with a loud *thunk*. "Does this have anything to do with Tanner Hughes moving back to town?" He actually sounds hopeful.

I look over at him. *"Daa-add."*

"You can talk to me about boys," he says.

"No. I can't."

"Of course you can! I am good at boys. I *am* a boy, after all."

I give him an ick face. "Ewww. Stop being gross, Dad."

"Would you just tell me if the smiles are about Tanner Hughes? Your mother thinks they might be. If you answer, I promise I'll go back to my reading."

"Okay, fine," I say. In what other situation does a father *wish* for his nearly fourteen-year-old daughter to be into a boy in a like-him, *like-him* way? Answer: only when said nearly fourteen-year-old daughter is a competitive gymnast, and Dad is hoping that she'll come around and see the sense in a normal social life. "It's true, I have been smiling a lot. But it has nothing to do with Tanner Hughes." I haven't seen Tanner since the Fourth of July, though I've looked for him down at the beach during my morning workouts.

Dad's face falls. "Really?"

"Really."

"Oh," he says, and so disappointedly too. "Well then, what *are* you so happy about?"

"Daa-addd!" I protest again.

"What? What did I do now?"

"You said you'd leave me alone if I answered your question, and I did."

"But you didn't tell me the reason."

"You specifically wanted to know if it was about Tanner Hughes — you didn't say in general."

"I'm your father! Don't you want your dad to know what's going on with your life?"

"Not particularly," I say, getting up from the couch. Whenever parents start referring to themselves in the third person, it's always best to get out quickly.

"Joey," he sighs.

"Dad," I mock sigh back. "If you want to know what's going on with my life, then you should come see me compete at Regionals."

He's silent now. Notice how my father can handle boy talk, but not conversation about the thing his daughter cares most about in the entire world?

I'm used to it. But I wish I didn't have to be.

"Bye, Dad," I say and cross the living room to the stairs.

"What's up with Alex?" Trish wants to know at practice the next day. We are on vault. Usually, I'd rather have to do nonstop belly beats on bars until my hips bruise and bleed than do a single vault, but lately I've been improving. I haven't kissed the vault once this entire week.

"I'm not sure," I say, even though this isn't precisely true. Practice has been underway for over an hour. Alex is not merely late today, I think she may not be coming at all.

Guilt stabs at my heart. I haven't yet told Alex what Maureen, Julia, and I are doing on Friday nights. It never seems like the right time. But she is my best friend, and the fact that I'm keeping something major from her, something that could affect my entire future as a gymnast, is a serious friendship violation, way worse than some gymnastics equivalent like stepping out of bounds on the floor exercise.

We just have an inverse relationship to gymnastics right now. The happier I get about it, the sadder and more frustrated she is.

Trish's eyes are wide. "If she's not careful, Coach is going to —"

"Trish!" Coach Angelo shouts. It's as though he has special

sensors in his head that let him know whenever we mention him at the gym.

"Yes, Coach?" she squeaks.

"You'd rather gossip than train? Is that it?"

"No, Coach."

He crosses the gym to stand next to the thick blue crash mat behind the vault, his muscular arms crossed and his eyes fixed on where we stand at the other end of the runway. "Then what are you waiting for?"

Trish knows better than to answer him. The only correct response is to salute the imaginary judges and start to run. Which she does. Unfortunately, her handspring into a full twist is so off center that she practically knocks Coach over, tumbling past him after her landing — if you could call running off the mat into the wall a landing.

Coach's expression, when Trish almost topples him, nearly makes me laugh out loud, and I have to put a hand over my mouth to cover the fact that I'm giggling. Trish is grinning herself as she heads back to the start of the runway. Like Trish before me, I smile at the invisible judges, then line up at the spot on the floor where I set up my run. It's marked JOEY with tape, which is a few inches farther back than the TRISH tape, but before the ALEX tape. The ball of my left foot pounds out my start, and in seconds, I am hitting the springboard and flying up and over the vault into a Barani — a somersault with a half twist — until I land on my feet, solid, my eyes level with the horse, arms behind my head.

Wow. If I vaulted like that at Regionals, I could even medal.

"Yeah, Joey!" Trish cheers.

I release my arms to my sides and turn to Coach for his assessment.

"Joey," Coach says, and I wait for it — the devastating remark about my lack of form, the flex in my left foot, the slight bend in my right knee, the microscopic twitch in my fingers. But he asks, "Is Alex all right?" as though he didn't see my vault at all.

Coach doesn't even sound angry. More concerned than anything else. I guess the Gansett Stars Darling gets her sins forgiven more easily than the rest of us. Gold medals win you at least that much.

In my mind I respond, *No. She's not all right. She's tired of practice day in and day out. She's sick and tired of the aching muscles and the endless hours of training. She's decided that it might not be worth it anymore. And by the way, I miss her like crazy.*

But I don't say any of this. Instead, I just shrug and walk back toward Trish, the smile on my face gone, trampled underneath my feet.

After practice ends, I half expect Alex to be waiting outside for me with an explanation and maybe even an introduction to Tommy. But she's not there when Trish and I push through the exit into the parking lot.

Instead, Tanner Hughes is in the grassy area next to the line of cars, bouncing a soccer ball from knee to knee to knee. He's wearing a green and white soccer uniform and Adidas sandals on his feet, with a black gym bag on the ground nearby. The door opens and slams behind me and Tanner turns my way.

"Joey," he calls out, catching the ball and tucking it under one arm. He picks up his bag and runs over.

My heart leaps as if it's on beam.

Trish gives me a nudge and a knowing smile. "Bye, Joey."

"But I thought we were heading home together," I say, giving her a pleading look. As much as I've wanted to see Tanner, now that he's in front of me, I'm nervous to be alone with him.

"Rain check," she says, and heads off.

Tanner stops a few paces away. His hair is a wavy mess. There is a smudge of dirt on the right side of his face and more streaks on his arms, his jersey, and across one leg. "Hey," he says.

"Hi. Did you have a game today?"

"Yup."

"Did you win?"

He grins. "We did."

"Cool. That's great," I say, then nothing else comes to mind. I don't know what to do next. "So . . . ah . . . what are you doing here?"

Tanner rolls the soccer ball from one side of his body to the other and back again. "I know you said you don't have time to hang out after practice — dinner and then bed and the same thing again the next day and all that."

I nod.

"But then I found out about *exceptions*."

I bite my lip, trying not to smile. "Like the Fourth."

"Exactly. So I've been thinking about what might count as *other* exceptions, and I figured, somewhere between practice and dinner you have to get home, right?"

"True," I say.

"So I thought I'd walk you and we can hang out on the way."

I find myself agreeing a little too eagerly. "Sure!" And we start to walk.

"I was thinking we could cut through here toward Main Street," Tanner says, his sandals scraping against the sidewalk.

"You don't want to walk by the ocean?" I ask, before I realize that this sounds like I am trying to get Tanner to take a romantic stroll on the beach.

His eyes are straight ahead. "Well, I wasn't entirely truthful when I said I was here to walk you home. At least not *directly*."

"No?"

He shakes his head, but he doesn't explain what he means, and his curls fall across his eyes in this way that makes me want to reach out and touch them. . . .

Get a hold of yourself, Joey!

A car honks at us as it passes and I jump. Mrs. Hamilton, our next-door neighbor, waves from the driver's side, so I wave halfheartedly back before turning to Tanner again. "You were saying?"

He hesitates. "Well . . . I was thinking we could stop at the diner for shakes. You know, like old times."

Um, *did Tanner just ask me out?* Because last time I checked, yes, it's true, we used to go to the diner downtown to get ice cream shakes when he lived here, but back then we went *with our mothers*. If I had to bet, I would guess that neither of our moms will be waiting in a booth when we arrive. *If* we arrive, since I need to agree to go in the first place for this to even be a possibility.

"Ah . . . yes? And no?" I say, torn about what to do.

"What do you mean, yes *and* no?" he says.

Oh gosh. "I *mean* that I'd love to go —"

"Great —"

I *have* to finish this thought. "— but also that my entire life revolves around gymnastics and, except for special occasions, you know, like on the Fourth of July as we've already established, all I do is train, practice, compete, hang out with my teammates, eat, and sleep."

"It's just hanging out and having shakes, Joey."

But is it?

"I'm not asking you to quit or anything," he adds.

Or maybe I just need to lighten up?

Tanner and I are stopped now, standing at the place where we would either head down to the beach on the way to my house or turn toward Main Street and the diner. He bounces the soccer ball once, then again, while he waits for my answer. There is a playful look in his eyes, which reminds me that this doesn't need to become a drama like it has with Alex. That, really, it's just hanging out and having ice cream shakes like Tanner said.

"How about next time," I suggest, thinking maybe a compromise is in order here. And also because I need some mental prep time for such an event, just like I do when I am about to perform on bars.

"Next time?"

"The next time you walk me home from practice."

His eyes light up. "So there will be a next time?"

"I guess so," I say with a smile of my own. "I just said there would be, didn't I?"

"You did," he agrees.

"So for today, we'll swing by the beach. Maybe take a walk?"

"Sounds good," he says.

We start on our way again and the conversation is easier now, as we talk about funny moments we shared in the past, his love of all things soccer, and why gymnastics means so much to me, among a million other things. It's the kind of back-and-forth that only old friends can pull off, even ones who haven't seen each other for a long, long time.

CHAPTER TEN

Delicious distractions.

It's Friday night, and Maureen and Julia are discussing the precise line of my body during one of the possible beginning poses of my floor routine.

Julia taps a finger against her chin. "If she just shifts the bottom half of her torso toward the right . . ."

". . . and her upper half to the left . . ." Maureen finishes, adjusting my shoulders so I manage just the right curve to her eye.

The two of them take a few steps away to observe their handiwork, while I stand there, frozen in this one position. Then they engage in further debate about the angle of my hand and the twist of my back, for what might be seconds, minutes, or hours for all I know.

My attention drifts elsewhere. Ever since Tanner walked me home, I've been thinking about him. Soon I'm imagining him sitting up in the imaginary stands at a meet, tense as he watches me compete at Regionals, all his focus on my every move, how amazing I am, how graceful and perfect. You know, that sort of thing.

A girl can dream, right?

"Joey. Joey!" Bright red-painted nails snap in front of my face. Maureen looks at me with exasperation. "Where *are* you tonight?"

"Sorry," I say, relaxing my muscles. I don't tell her where I am, for obvious reasons.

Maureen crosses her arms. "Did I say to come out of the pose?"

"No, Coach."

"Then what are you waiting for? Get back in position!"

Wow. Maureen can be more like Angelo sometimes than I expected. We only see her helping the younger kids at practice, being all sweet and encouraging, but she can bark when she wants to. I swing my left arm back up into the air with a flourish, the right along my back, chin tilted upward, eyes on the very ends of my fingertips, left leg planted firmly and the right stretched behind me, toes pointed — and *hold*.

"You need to have your brain in this," Maureen goes on. "Regionals is less than a month away!"

But hearing the word *Regionals* is like magic, and visions of Tanner cheering for me after a flawless beam routine dance in my head.

Julia's footsteps approach. "So during the initial notes of the music, she'll swing her arm down and around, meeting up with the other," she says to Maureen as though I'm not there. "And then on the first downbeat she'll do the jump."

"That's just what I was thinking," Maureen agrees.

"It's a beautiful pose — the judges will love it."

Maureen claps with excitement. "I know."

"With music this time?" Julia suggests.

"Yes, please," I murmur.

Their feet skitter off toward the stereo and soon the sounds of the beginning of my new and improved floor routine float into the air. I smile — I can't help it. I love everything about this new routine. As the music approaches the moment I am finally allowed to move, I shift out of the pose in perfect time, straight into the jump, and the beginning choreography.

Everything in life is better with music playing in the background.

And now my daydreams of Tanner have a soundtrack too.

Later that night, Julia drops me at home and speeds off to meet up with Madison and some other friends downtown. As soon as I walk in the door, I know something is wrong.

How do I know this?

Because my mother is grinning. No, maybe that's a smirk on her face. This means she has a secret and/or is about to embarrass me in some way.

Uh-oh.

"Joey! I'm so glad you're home. We have guests!" Mom beckons me to follow, taking a sip from her wineglass along the way.

Mrs. Hughes is in the living room, a wineglass in her hand too, a bottle sitting on the coffee table. "So nice to see you, Joey," she says. "Your mother and I are just catching up. Tanner's out back by the pool."

Tanner's here? Tanner's here!

"You should go say hi," my mother says with delight.

First Dad, now Mom. Apparently, both of my parents are not above trying to tempt me away from gymnastics with boys. Despite the smug look she wears, I don't argue. I just go. I've been thinking about Tanner all night, and now he's at my house, as if my daydreaming and wishing have conjured him up.

It's dark in the yard, except for the twinkle lights strung along the fence, and the soft glow along the bottom of the pool that bends and shifts with the movement of the water. The crickets are singing, but otherwise it is quiet. I don't see Tanner — not at first. Then I see feet, attached to knees, and I cross the deck over to him. He's sitting in a lounge chair, looking up at the stars, listening to his iPod.

I wave my hand in front of his face to get his attention.

He yanks out his earbuds and looks startled. "Oh hey, Joey." He sounds embarrassed. "This wasn't my idea, I swear."

It wasn't? Why not? I think to myself, realizing that I want it to be his idea and not simply our mothers'. "I'm glad you're here," I say and sit down in the chair next to his.

"You are? But I thought that with gymnastics —"

"I know what I've told you. I can still be happy to see you, though, right?"

Tanner looks at me, like he's trying to read my face in the darkness. "You're happy," he states, like he doesn't quite believe me.

"Um, yeah." Suddenly, everything is awkward with all of this admitting of gladness, and I want to fix that. Change the subject. "So . . . do you want to swim?"

Now he smiles. "Definitely."

"Be right back," I tell him, and run upstairs to change, avoiding our mothers along the way. When I return, Tanner is already in the pool, his hair wet, his eyes shining.

Oh. My. Gosh. I am about to go night swimming with a boy I think is really, really cute, who I'm pretty sure thinks I'm cute too.

I shouldn't be doing this. But I'm going to do it anyway.

Then I step up onto the diving board, walk to the end, bounce twice, and rise up, up, up until I twist with all I've got, driving back down so my body slices into the pool almost without a splash.

This is called *showing off.*

Shameless, yes. But at the moment I don't care.

"Wow," Tanner says, when I emerge from under the water.

I'm glad it's dark out or he would see that my cheeks are burning. "Alex and I do tumbling drills off the diving board all the time," I say to try to explain away my grand entrance. "Your turn."

Tanner grins, then launches himself out of the pool. "Okay. I'll be doing a double-back full twist into a spiraling somersault," he calls out as he runs around the edge, across the board and straight back into the water with a cannonball that creates a giant splash. When he comes up from the bottom, he's laughing. "So what's my score?"

I'm too busy wiping the water from my face and eyes to answer right away. "Um, I'll give it an A for effort?"

"I meant my gymnastics score!"

"It's difficult to know how to rate cannonballs," I say, smiling and shoving a wall of water toward him.

"But I was hoping for gold," he says, and swims closer.

"Maybe next time. I think you need to train harder."

Tanner and I are only inches away, treading water in the deep end, staring at each other, the slurp and gulp of the water as it hits the sides of the pool the only sounds aside from the crickets. My heart is pounding.

What happens next?

Apparently, me acting like I am still nine years old, since I propel myself up from the water with all the momentum I can muster so I can dunk Tanner — doing my best to evade his grasp once he gets his bearings — and swim away to the other side of the pool. I turn and see him shooting toward me underwater, his body a smooth line racing across the glowing blue bottom. He comes up just shy of where I am.

"Jordan, I did not see that coming," he says, shaking the water from his face and hair. "Retaliation is imminent." He lunges for me.

I quickly sidestep him, both of us laughing, shouting, chasing each other around. After we've gotten enough revenge for subsequent dunkings, we turn to other activities, like talking, and trying to see how long we can hold our breath underwater, and doing handstands on the bottom of the pool. We float on our backs and stare at the moon. Then we practice diving. Tanner wants me to teach him how to do a full twist off the board, though it becomes clear fairly quickly that this will not happen in a single night. I call out advice and direction about lift and rotation, but after yet another sideways crash into the water, Tanner gives up.

He swims over to meet me in the shallow end. I'm still giggling when he comes up. "Don't laugh, Ms. Perfect Gymnast."

"I can't help it," I say, laughing harder. "You should see yourself."

"Yeah. Well."

"Wow, great comeback."

I'm still laughing when Tanner leans toward me and looks into my eyes, the trace of a smile on his lips.

He hesitates.

And then he kisses me.

It happens so fast but oh my God it happens.

He pulls back quickly. Watches my face.

I am shocked, elated, swooning all at once. My heart is racing so hard I'm sure it will burst from my chest. "Tanner, I —"

But he cuts in before I can finish. "Can I do that again?"

"Yes" is all I say.

This time, the kiss isn't quick. It's slow and gentle, with time enough for Tanner and me to tilt our heads just slightly and part our lips a little. That we are in the pool in my backyard, swimming at night falls away. That our mothers are inside the house sharing a bottle of wine doesn't matter. Gymnastics, all that it means, my hopes about winning gold, they disappear too. I am dizzy, zinging with energy, the kind I thought only possible from flipping and flying across the floor or on the beam.

"Tanner?" Mrs. Hughes calls out suddenly, and we spring apart. She is on the back deck, looking into the darkness of the pool area. "We're leaving in a minute, honey."

"Okay, Mom," he calls back. "Be right there."

We hear her footsteps and the scrape of the sliding door opening and closing.

What now? There is a smile plastered on my face, but I can't look him in the eye.

"Joey?"

"Hmmm?"

"I guess I've got to go," Tanner says, his voice almost a whisper. "I wish I didn't."

"Me too," I whisper, and I mean it. "I'm going to stay in here and swim a while longer. Then I can avoid facing our mothers."

"Lucky you."

We stare at each other again. How do you say good-bye to the boy who just gave you your first kiss?

"So . . . ?"

"I'll see you soon," Tanner says.

"Yeah?"

"Next time for shakes. Remember?"

After tonight, how could I forget? "I remember."

Tanner smiles. "Good."

And then I think: *I just kissed those smiling lips!*

I smile back. "This was fun."

"Yeah, it was," Tanner says with another grin, and then pulls himself out of the pool, grabbing a towel to dry off. He picks up his flip-flops and his T-shirt, and throws the towel over his shoulder. Before he enters the house, he turns back one more time and looks out at me from the deck, to where I am still bobbing up and down in the water. "Bye, Joey," he says, and I can hear the laughter shining in his voice.

Up in my room, as I get ready for bed, my mind races, going over the kiss once, twice, a million times.

I can't stop thinking about it.

I can't stop wanting to kiss Tanner again, like, this very second. As soon as possible, at the very least. My head is swimming with Tanner, Tanner, Tanner Hughes.

And I learn something new about wanting something. In gymnastics, I want so much: the perfect routine, sticking the most difficult moves, wowing the crowd and my teammates and my coaches, and of course, winning gold. The desire for gold is insatiable. But tonight I feel want for something different, for a boy, for another kiss, for what that kiss made me feel because I want to kiss Tanner all over again. And again.

I'm so caught up in Tanner that for the first time in as long as I can remember, I don't bother saying good night to Nadia, Dominique, Nastia, and Ecaterina.

Tonight, I found out that there are other kinds of magic.

CHAPTER ELEVEN

Disappointments.

Things go downhill from there.

On Saturday after practice, the second I leave the gym, my eyes scan the parking lot, searching for the boy who I can't seem to stop thinking about, now that I've allowed myself to start. But I don't see that wavy, longish hair, that green and white soccer jersey, and that grin that has me swooning. I'd assumed Tanner would be waiting for me today, that the kiss we shared last night somehow meant that we would automatically see each other every day; that when we decided *next* time we would go for shakes at the diner, we meant *after my next practice.*

"Are you okay, Joey?" Trish asks, coming up behind me.

I bite my lip. "Yeah. I guess."

"Do you want to walk home together?"

"Sure," I say. Maybe he forgot I have practice on Saturdays.

As Trish chatters on about her predictions for Regionals, I am distracted. I can't think straight. I want to talk to someone about everything that is happening to me, all that is changing and so quickly. Someone who knows me better than everyone else in the world.

Where is Alex when I need her?

If she were here, I would finally confess to her about Tanner and my daydreams and how we kissed last night. I'd tell her all about my new floor and beam routines too. And then we could discuss the possible reasons why Tanner would kiss me last night and not show up today, analyzing every detail and feasible explanation, and I could feel comforted by my best friend.

I love Trish, but it's not the same.

On Monday, the same thing happens again: no Tanner. Tuesday's practice goes by, only to lead to disappointment when I leave. By Wednesday, I'm prepared for the day to end in frustration, but this kind of anxiety throws me off my game. I fall on beam. I fall on bars. I practically kill myself on one of my vaults. The only event I don't mess up — at least not as badly as the others — is floor.

How could Tanner do this to me?

Doesn't kissing, like, mean you're going out?

I want it to! So badly! Even though it could get me kicked off the team.

I'm starting to understand Alex's recent behavior a little better.

She hasn't been at the gym this week either, and she hasn't been in touch about why. It's not as though Alex and I have a plan in place for what to do if we aren't at practice together because we're *always* at practice together. This not talking at all is new territory for us.

"Joey Jordan!" Angelo barks from across the gym. "Focus!"

I am back on beam, trying to stick something. Anything. But nothing sticks. My feet are totally unstickable. I wish for Spider-Manlike sticky soles but to no avail. Once again I set up the back handspring, back handspring into a back layout, but I can't even land the first back handspring and I come tumbling onto the mat. Slowly, I pick myself off the ground.

"I don't care if you're up there all day and night," Coach shouts from his place near the bars, where he has a clear view of all four events while we practice. "You are to stay right there until you stick that pass!"

Here we go again. Imprisonment on the beam.

My shoulders slump, my stomach caves, and I am tempted to sit down and curl up into a ball until lights-out at the gym tonight. I can't deal with this right now. It sounds easier to wait out Coach's rage than keep going. I inhale deeply to say his name, but before I can even get to the *O* at the end of *Angelo*, he's yelling at me again.

"Don't even, Joey! Don't even. I don't want to hear it. You could be the best in the state, the best in the *region*, if you'd just get over these ridiculous hang-ups about tumbling! Just *do it* and don't complain about it!"

Yeah, well, I want to shout, *maybe if you didn't imprison me on a single event doing a single move the whole practice, I wouldn't develop hang-ups!*

But of course, I don't say this out loud.

Both of my hands hover over the beam as though I am trying to cast a spell on it. Then I press them down, propelling my body upward until I'm standing on it once more, trying to ready myself to throw this pass *again*. Sometimes I can't believe that beam is my favorite event. On days like today, it seems a rather painful choice.

Trish is suddenly in my line of sight, positioned in the far right corner of the floor exercise. She rolls her eyes and shakes her head, and I know she is telling me without speaking, *Don't listen to Coach. He's being unreasonable.*

Alex's voice pops into my head too, and the words I know she would be saying to me if she had actually shown up for practice: *We should quit. We should just quit and get this over with now.*

But the thing is I can't. I won't. Despite the fact that this week has been full of disappointments, it's only one week. Next week, *next practice* even, things will get better again. So I shake off the fear and frustration. I throw my shoulders back, head high, take two steps forward, and extend my arms so the tips of my fingers are my focus. I am ready to do this. Again.

"That's it, Joey! I knew you had it in you," Coach cheers when he sees me set up. I throw myself into the first back handspring, then straight into the second that is supposed to lead into my back layout, but my foot catches weirdly, my arms are suddenly flailing, balance gone, and I crash into a heap of limbs on the royal blue mats.

"Get up," Coach calls, his voice even but booming. "Again. Now!"

On Thursday, things go from bad to worse.

If that's even possible.

Midway through practice, Coach Angelo says, "Ladies, come gather. I have a surprise for you today!"

Sadly, this surprise is not birthday cake for someone or pizza for everybody or even new team leotards. Instead, Sarah Walker and Jennifer Adams march through the doorway like they own the place, followed by the rest of the Jamestown Gymcats. I shake my head and blink my eyes a few times, but Sarah and Jennifer and everybody else are still there when I open them. Cue the doom music.

"All right, everybody," Coach says, gathering us around him in a huddle.

The Gymcats stand off to the side, peeling off their warm-up jackets and shorts and beginning to stretch. Byron Thomas, their head coach, towers above even the tallest girls. Next to me, Trish keeps glancing over at them nervously. When Maureen catches me staring at them too, she gives me a face that says *Pay attention to Angelo, Joey.*

Coach says, "I thought you all could use a little pre-Regionals push, so I invited Byron to bring his team here for practice today. He and I took the liberty of pairing you up."

A couple of girls gasp — the way I feel too. The Gansett Stars *hate* the Jamestown Gymcats. Everybody knows this. What is Coach thinking? Does he want us to kill each other? Does he think this might thin out the competition at Regionals?

"I expect *all* of you," Coach continues, referring to the entire team yet looking specifically at me for some reason, "to be mature about this *and* to take advantage of this opportunity."

Opportunity? Seriously?

Coach takes the clipboard from under his arm and begins to read. "Alison, you'll work out with Katie Janson."

Alison groans. Coach gives her a look that will shut up any complaining instantly. "Tanya, you're with Beth Bronski. Heather, you're with Agnes Delmano," and so on and so forth.

Trish gets stuck with Jennifer Adams — poor thing. Meanwhile, I'm ticking off the rosters of both teams in my head, and with each name Coach reads, the dread intensifies until I know exactly what's coming.

"Joey, you're with Sarah Walker. I want you two to start on beam."

This is officially the worst week of my gymnastics life. This includes that time when I was twelve and I developed five rips on each hand, including two excruciatingly painful ones in the centers of my palms, and one rare thumb one, and the blood was flowing freely, and it didn't matter how much New-Skin I used or if I wore grips: My hands felt like they were on fire. When I dismounted from the most mind-numbingly painful bar routine of my life, I left four rings of red behind — two on the high bar and two on the low.

Yes, they were *rings of blood*.

Coach just told me that I needed to chalk up and go again.

Basically, what I am saying is this: Having to work on beam with Sarah Walker is the equivalent of doing bars with ten rips on my hands. Of having to stay on bars *indefinitely* with ten rips on my hands.

There is a snicker to my right. Sarah has heard the news that we are working together too. But of course, she takes it as an opportunity like Coach says we should — an opportunity to psych me out before Regionals.

After trudging over to the beam — well, I trudge; Sarah practically skips with glee — she turns to me with a wicked smile on her face.

"Johanna," she says. Sarah knows I hate my real name. "Do you want to go first? It is *your* gym, after all. Though maybe you'd like me to start? That way you can see what a gold medalist looks like when she's working out."

This is a disaster. That's all I have to say.

Sarah hops up on the beam like she owns it, her ponytail swinging jauntily behind her. "I guess you want to watch *me*, then." She does a switch leap with incredible height, then a quick pose, right into a back handspring followed by a back tuck, which she lands like the beam is the size of the mat below and not four inches across.

How does Sarah do that? Where does she get the confidence?

And she does it again. And again. She wants me to know that she is consistent. Without fears or hang-ups. That she can bang out leaps and flips on beam like they are nothing, and at a gym that isn't even her own, and in front of her rival too. (That would be me.)

But she's also a big hunk of muscular athlete, I notice — all brawn, no grace.

The one place where I'm confident about myself: I've got enough grace to support the entire team and the kind of flexibility that shows it off like nothing else could. It's my greatest strength and it's what's going to help me do a little intimidating of my own.

The fourth time she sticks the series, she crosses her arms, juts one hip out, and surveys the gym for a minute. "Hmm. I wonder where Alex is? Poor thing. Is that ankle injury still bothering her? Your team is really going to miss her scores at Regionals."

Could Sarah Walker be any nastier? Especially since the honest answer to her questions is *I don't know.*

But if Alex *were* here, she would have the perfect comeback ready to spit in Sarah's face. I wish with all my wishing might that I could summon Alex's attitude right now, that combination of sarcasm and biting wit that's a perfect match for mean girls like Sarah Walker and Jennifer Adams, but that never stoops to their level of low.

Then somehow, I do it.

"My turn," I say to Sarah. I hop up on the beam before she even has a chance to get down. *"Move,"* I tell her when she just stands there, staring at me like I might be possessed.

Maybe I *am* possessed.

Because what I do next seems to come from somewhere else, somewhere deep inside me that I'd almost forgotten. After Sarah jumps to the mat, landing with a heavy thud, I go into my favorite new series of moves on beam, the ones I've been developing with Maureen on Friday nights. First, I hit a series of pretty poses, including one that drops me to my knees, then I kick back into what looks like it will become a cartwheel. But then I drop my head below the beam, wrapping my arms around the bottom, my chin just below it, chest along the side, and my legs scissoring into a straddle split. I use this momentum to roll my way along the length of the beam in this same position — half turn, split, half turn, split — back and forth, until I'm almost at the end. After the last one, I straddle the beam, elbows down, swinging my legs straight up over my head until they are parallel with the beam. My toes are pointed, my back in a perfect C curve.

For the first time since Maureen started working with me on this creative, unusual pass across beam, I've done it flawlessly, and with the confidence and grace she keeps telling me she knows I have. I'm so pleased that I don't even pay attention to the fact that other people are watching, that my teammates might notice these new moves on beam. Or that Coach Angelo might see them too.

I just do it.

It feels great. *Right.*

After I hit my final pose, I relax, prop my chin in my hands, tilt my gaze toward Sarah Walker, and smile wide.

Sarah looks shocked.

Suddenly, Joey Jordan, serious gymnast, is back.

"Any questions?" I ask, batting my eyelashes at her.

CHAPTER TWELVE

Oh, the drama.

When I leave the gym after practice, I am beaming (so to speak), so caught up in the way things went from terrible to terrific that I don't notice the thick late July heat or that my hair is falling out of my ponytail or that tonight of all nights, Tanner is finally waiting for me outside. No, I truly don't notice this, at least not at first.

Then I do.

He's dressed in jeans and a T-shirt, as though he might be going down to the beach for the evening. Or, I don't know, on a date with me? My hand flies to my ponytail and I pull the elastic out, letting my hair down around my shoulders. Just like Serious Gymnast Joey showed up with Sarah, Boy-Crazy Joey is suddenly back.

"Hey, Joey," he says, coming over.

"Hi, Tanner," I say.

His hands are in his pockets and he looks nervous. "So I was thinking that today we could go to the diner."

I put my hand on my hip. My eyes narrow. "Why today?" I ask. I'm not going to make it that easy for him.

"What do you mean?"

"I mean, why not last Saturday or Monday or Tuesday or Wednesday? I had practice on all those days too."

He nods, his eyes on the blacktop. "I know."

"See, the thing is," I go on, my blood still pumping with confidence from showing up Sarah Walker, "when you said *next* time, I thought you really meant next time. As in, *next* practice. Then you didn't show up, so I figured you didn't really want to go to the diner with me after all. Or even see me again. Which hurt my heart after Friday night."

He opens his mouth like he might protest. Then he closes it again. Keeps staring at the ground. "I'm sorry, Joey."

"Yeah?"

"I just thought —" he starts, then stops.

"You just thought what? That Friday wasn't that big a deal? That you could show up whenever you feel like it, since I'm always here and you know how to find me?"

"No, that's not it."

I look at him hard. "Then what? Tell me."

"Well, I figured that since you've been very clear you don't really have time to hang out with me, if I showed up again the very next day, you'd be mad."

"You thought I'd be *mad*?" In all my obsessing over Friday, this possibility hadn't occurred to me.

"And I didn't want to look stupid," Tanner goes on.

"Stupid?"

"You know, too eager or something."

No, I don't know. Tell me more.

"So I tried to space things out a bit," he says. "Put a few days between last time we hung out and my showing up here."

He tried to space things out. Which means his absence was not from a lack of consideration or uninterest, it was from his caring *too* much about what *I* would think. Which makes his *not* showing up for the last few days kind of sweet. Wrong, but with sweet intentions at least.

His mouth twists. "Does this mean you don't want to go to the diner?"

"No," I say, a smile forming on my face. "I think it means I *do* want to go. On one condition," I add.

"What's that?"

"That this time, if we decide to hang out again, we also decide when and where before we say good-bye."

Tanner's grimace turns into a grin. "Deal."

"Good," I say, as we make our way out of the parking lot together. "Because gymnasts don't know how to play games, not socially at least. We never have the time to practice that stuff, because we're so busy practicing everything else."

"I think gymnasts may not be alone in that," Tanner says as we turn down the street. "But that's just a guess."

When Tanner and I walk in the diner, the first person I see is not the hostess, but Alex. With the boy I presume is Tommy. And she sees me too.

We stare at each other in shock.

Here we are, together again, yet not. *With boys.* Looking as though we're both on dates. And we are, kind of, aren't we?

She wants to smile, I can tell. After all the things I said to her about how she was risking her career as a gymnast and her place on our team by hanging out with Tommy, here I am doing the exact same thing. It's written all over her face that she's happy to suddenly have a partner in crime, and that this partner is me, of all people.

It's not what you think, Alex! It's just ice cream shakes! I want to yell, even though, yes, it totally is what she thinks, while another part of me wants to yell, *Alex, oh my God I totally kissed Tanner on Friday! With tongue!* But I don't shout any of this, of course.

Tommy doesn't seem to notice what's going on with his girl-friend, or whatever Alex is, since he is busy sinking his teeth into a Gansett Burger with all of the toppings. I can spot one from a mile away because I'm not allowed to eat them. *Heart attacks on a plate*, my mother calls them.

"I might want a burger with my shake," I tell Tanner. If I've gone all rebel without a cause, and I'm at the diner with a boy on a maybe date, then I may as well take advantage of the damage already done, right?

"I'm pretty sure they allow that here," he says.

And I laugh.

Alex gets up and heads toward us. She's smiling, but when she gets close, I can see guilt in her eyes. "Hey, Joey."

"Hey, stranger," I say back.

Tanner nods. "Hi, Alex."

"Do you guys want to join us?" Alex asks.

I try to raise one eyebrow skeptically, but I think they both go up. At least I tried. "By *us*, do you mean you and Tommy?"

Alex rolls her eyes — not a big roll, but enough that I can tell. "Yes, Joey."

Tanner looks from Alex to me. "Cool, then I'll just go have a seat while you two catch up," he says in one big rush, practically jogging away to join Tommy, who is still going to town on that burger.

"Where have you been?" I hiss.

Alex responds with a smirk, "Says the girl on the date."

"I'm not the only one on a date." But I'm not ready to admit being in a datelike situation, so I backtrack. "And I'm not even on a date. You're just misreading this."

"Uh-huh," she says disbelievingly.

"It's just ice cream shakes," I try.

"Uh-huh."

"Why haven't you at least texted to tell me what's going on?"

"Communication goes both ways, Joey."

Guilt knocks into me. Alex is right. I haven't exactly been forthcoming either. "Are you quitting?" I ask, and not simply because I want to change the subject, but because I really want to know the answer.

Alex sighs. "Can we talk about this later?" she asks. "This is really hard for me, Joey. It's the hardest decision I've ever faced." She looks like she's going to cry.

"Alex," I say, then stop. Even with all the tension between us, my heart breaks hearing those words from her. It breaks because I know it's the truth. If it were *me* in Alex's shoes, I don't know that I could stand up underneath all that weight.

So instead of pushing Alex further, I lean in and give her a long hug.

And just like that, I know that things between Alex and me will be okay no matter what happens. Boys and quitting are no match for best friends.

"Ice cream shakes, right?" she says after a while.

"Yup. And burgers too."

Alex looks surprised.

"Maybe," I add. "I'm considering ordering one."

"Good thing your mother isn't around to hear that."

"I know," I say and follow her to the table, where Tanner and Tommy are waiting.

I'm squished into a booth next to Tanner, across from Alex and Tommy, who is on his second Gansett Burger, because he sure can put them away. We're sipping ice cream shakes and acting like this is all perfectly normal — Alex and me hanging out with two boys in public at the diner. Like we might do this all the time or something. The conversation is going okay, and I even like Tommy too. I don't know that I like him enough to warrant Alex quitting her lifelong dream of being a National Champion for him, but he seems like a nice guy, in a jockish, older boy, *I'm Tommy and I drive a truck* sort of way. And he clearly likes Alex, which is important.

But then.

Julia walks in with her friend Madison and a bunch of other people. Girls, guys. A crowd of them.

"Hey, look, there's Joey," says a voice I recognize as Madison's.

"Where?" my sister says, sounding distracted. Then, *"Oh."*

This is not a good-sounding *Oh* either.

Which makes me respond, *Uh-oh,* inside, even though I'm not doing anything wrong, right? I mean, I'm just having shakes with friends — *isn't that what everyone agrees this is?!*

"Hey, Julia," Alex says.

"Hi, Alex," Julia says, her voice friendly but not *completely* friendly. She's standing by our booth, watching me.

Gah and double gah.

"Can I talk to you, Joey?" she asks. She is smiling, but her eyes say something else. Something particularly sisterly and judgmental.

"Um, sure," I say, getting up to follow her outside. The air feels warm and sticky after the cool temperature of the diner.

Julia grips my arm. "What are you doing, Joey?"

"What does it look like?" I hiss. "I'm having shakes with my friends at a diner. It's not a big deal, so *calm down.*"

I keep telling myself this to make this situation seem okay, but it sounds hollow when I repeat it to my sister.

"Is *he* the reason you were so out of it last Friday at practice?"

"No," I protest, but the very emphasis in my voice gives the real truth away.

"You shouldn't be here," she says. "Not like this."

"Like what?" I ask, even though I know what she means.

Julia's expression softens. "Listen, Joey, I know it's difficult — believe me, if anybody knows, it's me. You think it's not a big deal to be here, hanging out after practice one day — *just once*, you told yourself, right? That it's not a big deal to be on a date."

I open my mouth to protest again, but she silences me with her hand.

"And I know that you're *telling* yourself that it isn't a date, but this is how it starts."

"How *what* starts?"

"How what Alex is going through starts," she finishes.

"How do you know what Alex is going through?"

Julia tilts her head. "Believe me, it's obvious."

"It is?"

She nods. "Well, I've seen Alex hanging around that guy a bunch lately. And I know what's she's going through because I went through it once too. There was a time when all I wanted to do was quit. Because of a boy."

My jaw drops. *"What?"*

Julia purses her lips but doesn't say anything.

It's impossible. Aside from her injury — *despite* it — my sister sailed straight through her gymnastics years without a hitch and right on up to the top of the podium at Nationals. Hers was a gymnastics fairy tale. That's how everybody remembers it. "You thought about *quitting*? You almost had a *boyfriend*?"

"Yes."

"Who?" I can't help asking.

"Who it was doesn't matter," she says. "What matters is that it made me realize that if I wanted my dream to become reality, then the sacrifices were necessary. And that I could wait a few years for boyfriends. You know, that boys would still be there after I won gold."

There are tears in my sister's eyes. I blink back a few of my own. Julia never talks to me this way, especially not about her career as a gymnast. Her life always seems so breezy and perfect. "And *was* he?"

Confusion crosses her face.

"Was the boy still there after you won Nationals?"

"It doesn't make a difference," she says, but from her tone I don't believe her. Julia goes on before I can press any further. "You need to make a choice, Joey. Do you want to be the girl who wins gold? Or the girl who has a nice run for a while and then gets asked to homecoming?"

I shift from one foot to the other, then back again. "Can't I be both?"

Julia shakes her head. "Sadly, no. Really, you can't. Trust me. There's a reason why gymnasts aren't supposed to go out with boys. The drama is too distracting. At your level of competition, distractions can injure you permanently, or worse. And they certainly won't help you get gold."

I don't say anything. Not yet.

"So what is it going to be, Joey? At some point, some point *soon*, you are going to have to decide."

I open my mouth, close it, open it again.

Then I just shrug and turn away, leaving my sister standing there, waiting for an answer.

When I go back inside, I slide into the booth next to Tanner and take a long pull on the straw in my shake, pretending like nothing happened in my little talk with Julia, as if she's not staring at me from across the diner where she's rejoined her friends.

And everything is fine for a while. Really. For a few minutes longer, I can pretend that I'm the kind of girl who goes on non-dates. But then, my shake starts to taste melty and thin instead of yummy and thick, and the burger I ordered arrives and looks overwhelming and gross instead of juicy and tasty. Most of all, what Julia said begins to sink in.

I think about how much I messed up at practice this week, that tumble off the beam on Tuesday, how disappointed I was every single night when Tanner didn't show up. I think about how good it felt to do those new moves in front of Sarah Walker on beam today, not just wiping the smug look off her face, but *nailing it* once and for all, showing her and Coach Angelo and myself that I can be a top-level gymnast if I want to.

And I do.

Maybe the time for this — this Tanner and me thing — isn't now, no matter how much I like him, and no matter how much I want to kiss him again. Maybe some day, but not today, and definitely not if I want to win gold at Regionals and go on to Nationals.

And I want that too, more than anything else in the world.

More than hanging out with boys at a diner for sure.

Maybe even more than kissing Tanner.

Boyfriends are for other girls my age, not gymnasts. Not serious ones, at least.

Not me.

After we pay the check and say good-bye to Alex and Tommy, Tanner and I are alone again, standing on the sidewalk outside the diner.

"So . . ." he says with a smile. "What do you want to do now?"

A part of me, a *really* big part, screams *Kiss you!*

But I don't say this. I can't. Not even a hint of it.

Be strong, Joey.

I hesitate. Then I take a deep breath and say it. "Tanner, I had a really good time with you tonight, but I can't hang out anymore."

His smile disappears. "Do you mean you can't hang out anymore *tonight*, or ever?"

I close my eyes so I don't have to look at him while I do this, so I don't lose my nerve. "I *so* want to see you, like, every day. But I can't. I shouldn't. Not now, at least. Maybe after Regionals," I add, trying to make the situation better, even though I'm not sure that after Regionals, my life and priorities will somehow magically be different than they are now.

"But what if —" Tanner tries.

I open my eyes. I can't let him finish. "This is just the way things are right now. I'm sorry. I'm so sorry."

"Me too."

"As much as I want to be like some normal girl, I *have* to focus on gymnastics. Gymnastics is a full-time job."

Tanner looks away. Moves aside.

"Bye, Joey," he says.

"Bye, Tanner," I whisper.

I lean forward and give him a quick kiss on the cheek.

And then begin the long walk home.

Alone.

CHAPTER THIRTEEN

Facing the music.

Mom is the only one home when I get there.

"I'm out back," she calls when she hears the front door slam. "Come and say hello."

Having a chat with my mother is *not* what I feel like doing right now.

"Joey?"

Fine. "I'm coming."

I do my best to push thoughts of Tanner from my mind, replacing them with the memory of Sarah's stunned face earlier today after seeing my new moves on beam. This perks me up. A little. But only a little.

"Hi, Mom," I say, walking across the deck. She's lounging by the pool, tiny splotches of barium yellow dotting her arms. Maybe she's been painting suns today. I head down the stairs and join her on a lounge chair. The water sparkles and shifts, the blue along the bottom as blue as the evening sky. Being here reminds me of my perfect night with Tanner.

Ugh.

My mother puts her magazine down and shades her eyes against the setting sun, staring at me hard. "Are you okay?"

Am I? "Yes," I say. "I think so."

She cocks her head, gets that concerned-mom look on her face. "You only think so?"

I shrug.

She hesitates. "Do you want to talk about it?"

I shrug again.

She waits.

Can I talk to my mother about Tanner? Should I? Is that crazy?

She's still waiting.

Okay. "It's complicated, Mom."

"I can handle complicated."

I take a deep breath. "It has to do with Tanner."

Immediately, she smiles. "Oooh, tell me."

All the air comes out of me. "It's not like that," I say and before she can cut in, I go on. "I had to make a really difficult decision. You know . . . between Tanner and gymnastics."

"And?" The hope in her voice is obvious. She votes Tanner.

I look at her, annoyed. "I chose *gymnastics*. Because boys and gymnastics don't mix. And like Julia said, the boys will still be around in a few years, but gymnastics doesn't wait."

Mom frowns. "Your sister told you that?"

"Yes. And she's right. Gymnastics is everything to me right now. *Everything*," I say in one big rush. "I can't give it up for a boy. No matter who the boy is."

Then I stop. My mother has gone back to her magazine, automatically tuning out the minute I say how devoted I am to gymnastics, like she can't deal even with hearing about it.

"Mom?"

"Hmm?"

"Are you listening?"

"Of course," she says.

But she's not. "I thought you wanted to hear what I had to say. That you wanted to talk!" My voice is getting louder. She doesn't respond. "Mom!" I shout. "I was talking to you! You said you could handle complicated!"

"I'm sorry, sweetheart," she says, looking up again from the page. She sighs. "I just zoned out for a minute. Let's start again. Tell me what I missed."

"Everything, Mom," I say. "You miss *everything*."

That's what comes out of my mouth, and it sounds weightier than I originally intend. But given the fact that this is turning out to be the day of drama, I may as well get it all out, since tomorrow I need to get back to focusing on winning at Regionals. Period. No other distractions allowed.

She closes the magazine and places it on the table next to her, looking worried again. I have her attention. "What do you mean by that, Joey?"

"I know that Julia's time as a gymnast wore you and Dad out. I know that it was difficult to stick by her day after day, win or lose —"

"— or fall or injury or night of weeping," she interjects.

"Let me finish!" I shout, shocking even myself with such passion.

Mom opens her mouth, then thinks better of whatever she was going to say.

"I'm *your* daughter too, *and* I'm a *gymnast.* Like it or not. Falls and injuries and tears or not. Medals or not. The fact that you and Dad refuse to come see me compete bothers me more than I've ever said. It makes me hurt, that my own mother and father can't get up the guts to even *watch.* You realize that you don't know me at all, right? That you're abandoning me to do this alone? That you guys are the only parents who don't show? Do you realize you keep letting me down? Do you know all of this? Because I need you to. I need you to hear me."

Tears well in my eyes. I don't think I knew until this moment how angry I've been at my parents. Gymnastics may require sacrifices of me, hard ones, forbidding me a normal social life and time to hang out and goof off and Tanner and kissing and a million other things. But it *shouldn't* require me to give up the support of my family. That's just too much for me to handle.

"Joey," Mom says in a hushed, soothing voice.

"Don't *Joey* me!"

She purses her lips. Doesn't say anything else.

Maybe now she'll listen.

I do my best to slow my breathing before continuing on, my voice lower this time, so low it's almost a whisper. "I know you think you are protecting yourself from stress and pain, but if you guys don't get over this anxiety about seeing me do gymnastics, you're going to feel a whole different kind of pain, because you're not going to have been a part of the most meaningful thing in my life. Gymnastics is the *most meaningful thing in my life*, and I need you and Dad to deal with it." Her eyes are on me, steady. "I *love* gymnastics. I love it, heart and soul. And because you're afraid to watch, you don't ever see me at my best. Sometimes I hate you guys for that too."

Mom's eyes are glassy with tears.

My voice is hoarse. "I want you at Regionals. I *need* you there to support me. Please, please, please don't disappoint me on this." I watch my mother, trying to read her. "Mom?"

I wait for her to speak. To say she is sorry. Anything. But I get no response. I hang my head, sad, frustrated, exhausted by so much emotion.

Just then, Julia walks out onto the deck. "Is everything all right?" she asks, hesitant. "I just got home and —"

"No. It's not all right. And I was just leaving anyway," I say and take off.

When I get up to my room, I sprawl facedown on the bed. My sister's voice floats through the open window, then my mother's. They've obviously been talking ever since I left. At first, I cover my ears, trying to block them out, but then I decide I'd rather eavesdrop on their conversation.

"You guys aren't being fair," Julia is saying.

Mom sighs. "That's not true. Your father and I are *more* than fair to Joey. We made a deal with her, and she knew the terms from the very beginning."

"This isn't about paying the bills. Joey needs your support in other ways too."

"She knows we support her! Every time I write a check I'm supporting her."

"Mom!" Julia sounds frustrated. "It's not the same as being out in the stands at competitions so she can *see* your support."

"Julia, I simply *cannot* do it again." Mom sounds tired. Hurt by Julia's accusations, and mine. "I *cannot* handle the stress of watching another one of my children deal with that kind of pressure. It's inhumane, what those competitions do to you. I can't bear it. And that nasty Coach Angelo! I can't even be in the same room with him, let alone watch him scream at my daughter, and your father certainly can't handle it either, as he proved during your time as a gymnast. Every time I think of Joey on the beam or on bars or that godawful vault, all I can do is picture her crashing to the ground, over and over again, breaking her neck. I can't get these awful images out of my mind."

"Stop being so melodramatic," my sister shoots back. "Stop being so *negative*."

"Julia —"

"You should see Joey," my sister goes on before my mother can protest further. "She's amazing. You might be surprised how you feel when you watch her compete. I bet you'd forget all of that other stuff you're so worried about when you see her on floor and on beam. I'm not saying that you wouldn't feel *any* stress or *any* anger at Angelo or *any* worry about her feelings or whether she's going to get injured — that's still part of the deal. I get it. But I think you'd be proud of her. I *know* you would. I know I am, at the very least."

Julia thinks I'm amazing? She's proud of me? I guess Maureen's coaching really has made a difference.

I peek up from the comforter, lifting myself high enough so I can see through the bottom of the window. Mom wipes her eyes. She *is* crying.

Julia's not done yet either. "And is it really worth it, Mom," she goes on, "to give up feeling proud of Joey to save yourself some heartache? Doesn't even a little bit of your heart ache anyway? Because of what you're missing out on?"

"Have you been to see Joey practice?" my mother asks in a small voice, sounding sad but curious too. She sniffles a little. This might sound mean, but I'm happy that she's feeling guilty.

"I *have* been to see her," Julia says. "And I know I'm not a fortune-teller, but Mom, Joey is going to win Regionals this year. I know she is. I just do. And you and Dad *have* to be there for it. Just like you both were there for me."

I can't believe Julia said that, about me winning Regionals. And that she's fighting so hard for me here. Tears stream from my eyes. I reach up to the top of the window, closing it quietly. I've heard enough.

Then I slip on my flip-flops and leave the house, because right now, after all that has happened today, what I need most is a friend.

My *best* friend.

CHAPTER FOURTEEN

Fessing up.

When I arrive at Alex's house, she's sitting out on the front steps, peeling an orange and leaving the rind in a pile next to her. I stand in the grass of her front yard, waiting for her to see me. She looks up.

"Hey!"

"Hey," I say, walking up to her.

"So that was fun, you know, at the diner. With Tommy." Alex grins. "And *Tanner.*"

I take a deep breath. "About the diner . . . and Tanner."

"Tell me." Alex pats the space next to her on the steps, the side without the orange peel, inviting me to join her there. So I do.

"Tanner and I aren't happening. At least not anymore. Not now."

"Joey," Alex says, sounding sad. "He likes you. And you like him back! It's obvious."

My shoulders shrug. "I know."

"Does this have anything to do with Julia pulling you out of the diner to talk?"

"A little," I say. Then, "Yes. It was kind of a wake-up call. Julia said that I needed to focus, that boys are distracting, that boys were not for now but for later. And they'll still be there when I decide I'm ready to be done with gymnastics."

"You agree with her?"

"Well, kind of. Gymnastics provides enough drama in my life already. I don't need to go seeking more, and boys and drama are like, I don't know, inseparable. All that wondering if Tanner likes me or if he's going to show up or not after practice was really distracting this week when I was trying to stick my beam routine."

"But it's okay to like Tanner. I mean, it's *normal* to like boys. We're fourteen!"

"Yeah, but the timing isn't right. I need to focus."

"Did you tell him already?"

I nod, playing with one of the orange peels, the smell of citrus strong and tangy in the air.

"Oh, Joey."

"It totally sucks." I look at her. "Especially because I kissed him."

Her jaw drops. "You did not!"

I smile a little. "I did. Like, almost making out. We were in the backyard swimming at night."

"Oh, that's so romantic," Alex practically squeals. "So is he a good kisser?"

"Um, despite the lack of anyone to compare him to, I'd say yes."

"Wow. You kissed Tanner Hughes."

"I did. And now I don't get to kiss him again for who knows how long. Or maybe ever."

But Alex gets a dreamy look on her face. "Or . . . maybe he'll wait for you and someday, like, after you win Nationals or even better, *the Olympics* —"

I roll my eyes. Alex keeps right on going, though.

"— right after you've gotten the gold for All-Around — the Olympics are somewhere nice and dreamy too, by the way, like Paris. So as I was saying, you've just gotten the gold, the national anthem is finishing, and you come down off the podium and everyone is hugging you and throwing flowers because you're America's newest sweetheart, and giving you flowers too, and you look up and there's Tanner! And he's wearing an expression of undying love on his face —"

"Alex," I interrupt, even though I'm loving every word she says.

She holds up her hand. "I'm almost done!"

"Fine, go ahead."

"So he's got undying love on his face and you run to him and he runs to you and he picks you up and twirls you around and then you kiss in front of *the entire world* because it's broadcast on television, because this is the Olympics after all, and you are glowing and happy and Tanner is too, because you can finally be together." Alex smiles wistfully. "The end!"

"Are you sure?"

She nods, still smiling.

"What happens after the kiss?"

"Oh, I don't know. You guys go out for dinner or something."

I laugh. "I'll admit, it's a good fantasy."

"I know." She sighs. "I wish it could have been me and Tommy. Oh well."

"I don't understand. Why can't it be you and Tommy?"

Alex gets a faraway look on her face. Doesn't say anything.

"I thought he was nice," I go on. "I like him."

She lights up at this. "Really?"

"Yup, really."

"That means a lot," she says. Then she gives me a searching look. Picks up another orange from the bowl on the stairs and starts to peel it. She hands me one too. "Your sister's right, you know. About how boys and gymnastics don't mix."

I brace myself for what's coming next.

"Gymnastics and I are over," Alex finally admits.

I gasp, even though I was prepared. "For real?"

"For real," she confirms. "We've been over for a while. It's just taken a long time for me to finally admit it."

"But Alex, if anyone at our gym has a chance of winning at Nationals next year, it's you."

"It's not me anymore, though. It's not what I want."

I pop an orange slice in my mouth, chewing slowly, waiting to hear what she says next.

"Really, Joey. It isn't. I want dates with Tommy and kisses good night and a normal social life. Besides" — she lowers her voice — "I'm totally getting boobs!"

"What?! You are?"

"I am. I even had to go out and buy a bra. And you know what that means."

"That you'd look really hot in your leotard?"

She laughs. "But even better in a bathing suit."

"Wow," I say, taking her decision in. "Wow."

"Yeah."

"Thanks for telling me."

"I'm sorry I didn't sooner."

"It's all right," I say. Then I realize I have another confession to make. "There's something *else* I need to tell you."

Alex's eyes are curious. "What?"

"I've been doing secret Friday night practices at the gym. Maureen choreographed new floor and beam routines for me."

"No way! Coach doesn't know?"

I shake my head.

"Do you fear for your life? I mean, Maureen must."

"Honestly, I don't think she cares. All she keeps saying is, 'Joey, your talent was wasted on those other routines.'"

"Well, she's right," Alex says, her mouth full of orange.

"I know. I've always known. That's why I wanted this."

"So you like the new routines?"

I smile. "I *love* them. They're graceful and fun and peppy and they make me happy. And the music is pretty fantastic — none of that boring classical stuff."

Alex puts an arm around my shoulder. "You're going to win Regionals this year, Joey."

"I'd like that," I say, even though inside I'm thinking about how sad it will be to compete without her. "So . . . when are you going to tell Coach the news?"

Alex sighs. "I don't know. Soon. I mean, he's probably guessed by now. He's called the house a gazillion times and I haven't called him back yet."

"Do me a favor?"

"What?"

"Talk to him on a Sunday. Or at least wait till *after* practice is over."

She laughs. "I can probably agree to that. Oh, Joey," she adds.

"I know," I say. "I'm going to miss you so much."

"I'm going to miss you too." I lean my head on Alex's shoulder. She keeps her arm around me and we sit like this for a long time not saying anything.

"Things won't be the same without you," I say after a while.

"Not the same, no," Alex agrees as the last rays of sun disappear beneath the trees. "But we'll figure it out. Our friendship goes way beyond gymnastics, Joey. It always has."

That night, before bed, I go through my ritual. I kiss the palm of my hand and tap each of the posters with my four favorite goddesses of gymnastics, in all of their grace and gold medal glory — Nadia, Dominique, Nastia, and Ecaterina. "Come on, ladies. Lend me some of your magic," I say like always.

But for some reason, this night feels different. Alex's confidence that I'll win Regionals and Julia's calling me amazing scroll through my mind again and again. Their faith in me is having an effect on the faith I have in myself. And this might sound crazy, but tonight, I think that someday *I* could be one of the gymnasts featured on a poster, with girls looking up to me,

Joey Jordan. Just like I look up to Nadia and her fellow champions.

Just like other girls look up to my sister, Julia.

And then I do something I never believed I would want to do. I get up and go to my closet, digging into the far back, behind piles of forgotten clothes I don't wear anymore, to slip out a rolled-up poster from its exile in the corner.

A poster of Julia Jordan, U.S. national champion.

I tack it up on the wall next to the other gymnasts who have been my heroes ever since I started to compete. And as I drift off to sleep, I think that maybe, just maybe, winning gold medals runs in this family, and that someday, I'll know what it feels like to stand up on that podium for real.

I don't run away from a challenge because I am afraid.

Instead, I run toward it because the only way to escape fear

is to trample it beneath your feet.

— NADIA COMANECI, ROMANIA,

1976 Olympic All-Around champion

CHAPTER FIFTEEN

But I'm too young to die.

On the way out the door to my last Friday night practice before Regionals, I pass my parents, who are sitting at the kitchen table. Their expressions give me the sense that they were in the middle of a heavy conversation. I'd better get out while I can, so I reach for the doorknob.

"Joey," my father says. "Your mother and I were just discussing you."

I fidget, shifting my weight from one foot to the other. Now is not the time for a heart-to-heart with the 'rents, especially since Julia is outside waiting in the car. "What about me?"

"Sweetheart," Mom cuts in. She sounds nervous. "We were wondering how you would feel if we came to watch you compete at Regionals."

"Really?" I stand straight and still. Wow. Between telling Mom off by the pool the other day and Julia's guilt trip, it seems they're coming around.

"Yes, really," Dad says, his voice filled with hope.

They're trying to make it up to me, which means that even though I feel alone and angry sometimes, they care about what I do and want to be a part of it. At least a little bit. At least once in a while. Which makes me happy. Better late than never. Better something than nothing at all.

They look at me, anxious. "We love you," they say together.

"I know," I say, taking in their eager faces. "Of course I want you there at Regionals."

"Good!" Dad exclaims. "That's great to hear. We'll be in the stands then, cheering you on."

"I might have to cover my eyes now and then," Mom confesses.

"That's okay," I tell her. "Sometimes I want to cover my eyes too."

When I get in the car, Julia has my floor routine music playing over the speakers. She keeps listening and then skipping back to this one part.

"I think on that straddle leap," she says, her eyes on the rear-view mirror, "instead of having your arms to the side, you should extend them out in front of you, palms to the ceiling, fingers wide, like you're reaching for the judges. Big smile on your face, of course."

"Let's see what Maureen thinks."

"Just don't forget to ask her," Julia says as she backs out of the driveway. The sky is still pink on the horizon from the sunset.

"I won't." I grab the iPod and press pause. The inside of the car goes silent.

"Joey!"

"Calm down," I tell her. "There's something I want to tell you."

"Uh-oh."

"Not *uh-oh*," I say, mimicking her tone. Julia and I may be all buddy-buddy lately, but this doesn't change the fact that we're sisters and get on each other's nerves easily. "Mom and Dad asked if they could come see me at Regionals next week."

"Oh, they did?" Her face brightens at this news.

"Yes."

"And?"

"I told them to come, obviously."

"That's great. Really great."

Then all my concerns pour out. "But what if Mom can't handle it and rushes out of the stands, traumatized, and throws me off my game and then I mess up my event and fail to win even a bronze?"

"Joey, don't you think that's a bit melodramatic?" Julia says.

"No," I protest, even though it totally is.

"Mom will be fine."

"I hope so. At least she's trying. At least they both are."

"Exactly. Stay positive."

"Thanks for helping to convince her," I say, even though I'm not the gooey type.

"I think you did most of the convincing before I arrived," Julia says. Then she immediately gets back to business. She's not the gooey type either. "Enough parent talk. Time to focus, Joey."

"Yes, Coach," I say, only half kiddingly.

Julia smiles. "No one has ever called me that before."

"Don't get a big head. I was only joking. Mostly."

But Julia doesn't lose the smile as we turn down the road for the gym. "Maybe someday I'll be one for real," she says.

That night I go through my beam routine at least fifteen times.

I practice the mount and the dismount.

I practice the back handspring, back handspring, back lay-out sequence even more, not because of Angelo, but because I'm determined to keep it in my routine for me.

I work on the presses and the handstands and the poses and that awesome pass when my head is underneath the beam and my arms are gripping it and my legs are scissoring away above it — the same one that showed up Sarah Walker at practice the other day, and that emphasizes my strength and flexibility and poise and style. All those things that will help me kick her butt at Regionals from here to, I don't know, some remote island off the coast. Hopefully. It may not involve tumbling, but because of its degree of difficulty, it is worth *a lot* in terms of score.

I fall only twice the entire practice. Not bad, right?

On floor, my music plays over and over again, sometimes in its entirety, sometimes in pieces, with Maureen and occasionally Julia piping up to tell me to try my hands differently or shift my arm to a new angle or heighten my leap above their heads or some ridiculously impossible instruction like that.

But I smile the whole time.

I still think about Tanner in the imaginary stands. But only a little. Because I need to focus.

When I finish my last run-through of the night on floor, I come out of my final pose, beaming.

Julia whistles in appreciation from her perch on the vault.

"I think you're ready," Maureen says.

"I *feel* ready," I say.

Maureen walks toward me, her sneakers padding softly against the mat. "Good. Because tomorrow after practice, you're going to show your new routines to Angelo."

My jaw drops in shock. "What, are you crazy?"

"I second that," Julia chimes in.

"Joey," Maureen says, shaking her head. "Did you think this day would never come?"

"Um, kind of?"

"Well, it's here. You have to show Angelo, or you'll never be able to perform these routines at Regionals."

"You mean, this whole time you haven't had some other plan for how this would all come together?" I say. "You've always known I would have to show Coach Angelo, telling him that we've been going behind his back, giving him plenty of time to kill me?"

Maureen doesn't even flinch. "Joey, this isn't some movie where we dramatically overthrow the head coach," she says, like I should know this already.

"It isn't? Are you sure?"

"Positive."

I gulp. "Well, this has been amazing, and I want you to know ahead of time that it's been nice knowing you, and I really appreciate all the time you've put into helping me, and —"

Maureen sighs. "Joey."

"Yes?" I whimper.

"Calm down. It's going to be all right. Sometimes it's better to ask forgiveness than permission."

"What does that mean?"

"It's just a saying. Anyhow, I think we should address your fears."

Oh great. Now Maureen is being a coach *and* a therapist.

"What's the worst that can happen?" she asks.

"Um, death. I believe I mentioned that a moment ago."

"I want you to be serious now."

"I *am* being serious. You know how angry Coach Angelo can get, especially if we try to pull one over on him, and I think this qualifies as a massive pulling one over on him."

Maureen waits for me to provide another possibility.

So I concede. "Well, aside from death, which I think we all can agree is pretty bad, let's see . . . he could *fire* you and kick me off the team."

Maureen bobs her head, considering the idea. "Maybe. I doubt it, though. Angelo would be crazy to let you go."

"But —"

"No *buts*," she cuts in, not letting me protest. "You're his brightest star."

An image of Alex standing on the podium to get the All-Around gold medal at our last meet pops into my head. That competition feels so long ago now, with everything that's happened since. "*Alex* is the Darling of the Gansett Stars."

"I beg to differ," Maureen says. "I *always* have, Joey. I've always thought it was you. And don't forget, Alex hasn't been around."

"I know," I whisper, the knowledge of this truth still painful to face.

Julia hops down from the vault and joins Maureen and me in the middle of the floor exercise. "Do you two have any interest in what I think?"

"Go ahead," Maureen says.

I just shrug. Maureen is totally right: I don't know what I've thought all this time about what would have to happen to get us from secret practices and secret new routines to nonsecret ones that I would perform for other people, including Coach Angelo.

"Coach's possible *realistic* reactions could include the following," Julia begins, brushing her long hair back from her face. "Sure, he could fire Maureen," she says to me, and then to her, "or kick Joey off the team, but the chances of that happening are so slim we shouldn't even worry about it."

"That makes two of you, I guess," I mutter.

"Let me finish," Julia says. "What's more likely is that he will not allow Joey to compete at Regionals at all, and he won't let Maureen coach either."

This possibility makes me squeak.

"He won't do that, though. He can't. It would hurt the team's chances too much. Really, the worst possible scenario — and this is the one I think we should prepare ourselves for — is that he gets angry at you both for holding practices without telling him. Even that isn't too bad, though, since you, Maureen, can simply claim that Joey wanted extra help and time on beam and bars, and you agreed to be here while she worked out, and one thing led to another and now Joey has new routines. This is all perfectly plausible and forgivable."

"Maybe if you didn't know Coach Angelo, sure." I'm back to muttering commentary. I can't help myself. "But you do, so none of this makes sense."

"Joey," my sister says, looking at me hard, her hands on her hips. Julia may be tiny in that gymnast sort of way, but she can be formidable when she wants to be. "I'm betting that all Coach will do is say you have to perform your old routines at Regionals."

"But that would mean all of these Friday nights and my awesome new floor and beam are for nothing!"

"No, they aren't," Julia continues. "Because when the time comes at Regionals, you'll just do them anyway."

"But as soon as I disobey him and do one unauthorized routine, he's never going to let me do the other. Which one would you even pick? Or will it just depend on which event I compete on first?"

"Joey, we'll cross that bridge when — and *if* — we come to it," Maureen says. "Right now let's just think positive thoughts about Coach Angelo's reaction tomorrow. You never know — he might surprise you."

I put my arms around my head protectively, as though Coach's rage might overwhelm me already. "Oh, I know."

"Go home and get some sleep. You've got a big day tomorrow."

"That's one way of looking at it," I say as Maureen, Julia, and I walk toward the exit, leaving everything in darkness behind us.

CHAPTER SIXTEEN

Friends, maybe.

On Saturday morning, I wake up with a pit in my stomach. I have to tell Coach Angelo about my new routines today.

Gah. *Triple* gah.

The sun is already bright in the sky and the sheets are sticky. Mom must have turned off the air again, as if I needed another reason to sweat today.

There's only one sure way to calm down: go off to the beach for a swim before practice. I can follow the dip in the ocean with some circuit training to further clear my head, and *then* make a final decision about whether to go to practice or flee the country.

Because right now fleeing the country seems like the best idea, you know?

The water is surprisingly warm and I stay in longer than I originally plan, jumping with the waves, bobbing up and down, diving to the bottom, skimming along the ocean floor. For a while, I float on my back, thinking. I go over all the possible reactions Coach might have, according to me, Maureen, and Julia. The only possibility that we *didn't* discuss was the one where Coach falls so madly in love with my new routines that he forgives the sneaking around we've done all summer.

Interesting, isn't it? That this is the one outcome none of us could see happening? But it's a possibility too.

Eventually, I start to shiver, so I wade toward the shore. The beach has begun to fill up. Little kids dot the shallows and a couple of parents stand ankle deep, chatting with one another. An old man has set up a lounge chair in the wet sand where the waves keep rolling through, to keep cool on this sweltering August morning.

I dry off with a towel and do backflips down the beach to calm my nerves, but it's just not the same, flip-flopping without Alex. So I stop suddenly, the balls of my feet digging into the hard sand, my knees bent, absorbing the landing. I don't rebound because it's as though even my gymnastics is too stressed out to be normal today. Since forgetting about my life doesn't seem possible, I work on my shoulder strength with timed handstands, followed by sprints in the hilly, dry sand. Then I make my way over to a lifeguard chair so I can grab one of the wooden slats on the side. I rise up on my left toes, holding the position until my calves start to burn, then holding it some more until I switch to the right.

That's when I notice a group of boys playing soccer a few yards away. I take a good, long look in case Tanner is one of them.

He *is* one of them.

Tanner is running back and forth across the sand, pointing at players and shouting things like "Over here!" and "Stay on that defender!" He gets behind the ball now and then, or stands there for a minute, shading his eyes from the sun. His dirty blond hair is tied back into the shortest ponytail I've ever seen, though some strands escape and fall around his face, so he has to keep brushing them out of the way.

Oh, he's so cute, I think. Then I wish I didn't feel this way. *Then* I wish it didn't have to be so complicated, so it would be okay that I feel this way and not something I have to resist. By now I am no longer up on my toes, but simply standing in the sand, still gripping the wooden slat under the lifeguard chair, peering through to the other side like some weird beach stalker.

Should I turn around and sneak away before Tanner notices me here? Should I call out his name and see if he happens to hear me, and if he doesn't, take it as a sign that I'm not meant to talk to him right now and walk away? Should I waltz right up to him, making sure he notices me, and act like I didn't leave him outside of the diner the other day in a melodramatic fashion? Or should I waltz right up to him and *directly address* what happened after we left the diner and why I did what I did?

Regardless of what the best plan is, I know one thing for sure: I want Tanner and me to at least be able to talk.

A surge of courage rises up inside me, and I emerge from my hiding place behind the lifeguard chair and head over to wait and watch the players.

It's not waltzing, but still.

I am going to talk to him, give him more of an explanation. I *am*. I owe him this much. I owe me this much too.

There is a time-out in the game. This is my chance. "Tanner!"

His head snaps my way. "Joey?"

I give him a little wave.

He turns to the other players and says something that I don't catch, then runs in my direction.

"Hi," I say when he gets here. But nothing else. I am nervous.

"Hey," he says, but nothing else either. Maybe he's nervous too?

What next? Where to from here? Where's that familiar grin of his? He's not smiling now. He stares at me as though he's waiting for me to say something. His eyes are sad.

I take a deep breath. "I'm sorry about the other day."

"Sorry how?" he asks. "Sorry and you've changed your mind and want to hang out, or just sorry that nothing has changed?"

"The second one," I say, even though it's difficult when I am this close to him, and all I can think about is leaning in and kissing his lips. "Tanner, I *can't* go on dates."

"But we agreed it wasn't a date," he responds automatically. "It was just ice cream shakes. Well, and you had a burger."

"Can we at least agree it was *datelike*, then?"

Tanner smiles a little. "Yeah, I suppose."

"The thing is, I can't do datelike either. Not right now, and especially not with a boy I've been kissing. I think the kissing stuff is what, um, made things more datelike in general. At least for me."

Did I really just say that out loud?

Now Tanner grins. "I thought you liked the kissing. Seemed that way, at least."

My cheeks are in bloom. I stare at the sand. "I did. I do. Which is exactly why I can't keep doing it."

"But that doesn't make any sense," Tanner says.

I make myself look at him again. "Gymnasts can't afford distractions."

The waves crash and pull away, crash and pull away, providing a soundtrack to our little heart-to-heart.

"I'm a distraction?"

Honesty is always the best policy, so I go for broke. "Listen, Tanner," I begin. "You totally *are* a distraction. I can't be thinking about whether or not you want to hang out with me while I'm trying to land a vault or stick my beam routine. I can't even be thinking about how I'm *certain* you want to hang out with me and how nice that is. And I *definitely* cannot be thinking about kissing you while I'm doing anything remotely gymnastics related!"

Tanner's grin gets bigger, if that is even possible. "You've been thinking about kissing me that much?"

I don't bother to answer this, just give him a look. "The *only* thing I can be thinking about while I'm at practice or a meet is the task at hand. I need total focus. Gymnasts have it tough enough as it is, with all of our hang-ups and fears and other people psyching us out and saying nasty things while we're competing. We don't need to add boy drama to the mix."

Now Tanner's giving me a look. "I count as boy drama?"

"Well, you *are* a boy."

"Glad you noticed."

"Would you settle for counting as good boy drama? Or even as a good distraction?"

Tanner is trying hard not to laugh. That's how I know that somehow everything will be okay. "I might," he says. "It depends, though."

"On what?"

"Are you allowed to be friends with boys? Like, with me in particular?"

I have to contemplate that for a minute, so I do. *Can* I be friends with Tanner? I mean, can anybody truly be friends with someone she thinks is really cute and wants to kiss all the time and about whom she entertains daydreamy fantasies that involve the so-called friend looking adoringly at her while she wins gold medals? Isn't friendship a bit torturous once day-dreamy fantasies become part of the picture?

Maybe.

But maybe it's worth it?

"Can we come back to this question after I compete at Regionals?" I ask.

"When is Regionals, exactly?"

"In four days. On Wednesday."

"Oh. That's not so far."

The reminder that Regionals is just around the corner makes me queasy for a moment. "No, it really isn't."

"Are you okay?" he asks.

"Yeah. Just nervous when I think about it."

"So Regionals is a big deal."

"Kind of. Wait, what am I saying? Yes. It totally is. I have new routines too. And gym drama to go along with them."

"Gym drama?"

"It's different than boy drama. But *all* drama is distracting and messes up a gymnast's focus, which is not good."

"Can you solve the drama? You know, make it so it's not a drama anymore?"

I think about showing Coach my new routines today after

practice, trying to decide if this is a method for drama solving. My mind can't quite wrap itself around this possibility, but I say, "Maybe," anyway.

Then Tanner asks a question I am not expecting. "What happens if you do well at Regionals?"

"I get really happy," I say.

"Well, obviously. But what else?"

I think for a while. What else *does* it mean? "If I win at Regionals, then not only will I be happy, but I qualify for Nationals. At the very least, it will get me noticed in the gymnastics world, and say to people that my gymnastics career has potential beyond just the ordinary."

"Like to be extraordinary?" Tanner asks.

"Kind of."

"Wow. So I *may* be friends with someone who *may* be good enough to win at a national level."

I laugh. "You *may* indeed be. But that remains to be seen."

"I guess so," Tanner says, his eyes thoughtful. "Can I ask you one last question?"

"Sure," I say.

"If gymnastics requires so much sacrifice, and makes your life so complicated, then why do you keep doing it?"

I look at him. "Because sometimes, very rarely, but once in a while, you have this rare perfect day when you win — maybe you win it all," I say, remembering the day this happened for my sister at Nationals. Picturing it. "And winning is not only glorious, it helps remind you why you love this sport so much, since it's also really, really fun."

"I can understand that, I think," he says. He glances over his shoulder at his friends, who are playing soccer again, one man down. "I should get back to my game."

"Okay. I'm glad you came over to talk."

"Me too." Before I know what's happening, he leans forward and plants a quick kiss on my lips. "Good luck at Regionals, Joey. I really, really hope you have that perfect day."

And then he is gone.

A big smile breaks across my face, my cheeks turning a red as deep as the stripe on my team leotard. I know I shouldn't care, that I should turn my attention to serious subjects like practice and the stuff with Coach, but I spend a good long time going over this moment with Tanner. Then I think about Alex's over-the-top vision of Tanner showing up after I win the Olympics and us having a glorious, world-televised kiss. I decide to tuck away this daydream for safekeeping, because even if it's a silly fantasy, I still kind of like contemplating it.

I can't help it either.

I may be a serious gymnast, but I'm a girl too.

CHAPTER SEVENTEEN

Moments of reckoning.

At practice I remain in a low-level state of fear because I'm in the same room as Coach Angelo. This doesn't help me perform well, to say the least.

"Joey!" Coach barks from the other side of the gym, where he is standing by the bars. "What are you, a grandmother? If you run any slower down to the vault, we're going to have to put you in a wheelchair!"

"Joey!" he barks again a while later, from where he's watching my teammates on the high beams. "If your cast handstand on high bar gets any weaker, we'll have to hire a crane to pull you up at Regionals!"

Coach has eyes everywhere. It doesn't matter if he isn't watching you specifically, he still sees all. And he's not even trying to be funny. He's dead serious when he says this stuff.

"Joey," Coach seethes after I've landed my bars dismount, bouncing all over the mat before I come to a halt. "If you don't tighten up, they're going to sell Joey Jordan bobble-head dolls in your honor!"

Maureen keeps coming over to check in and try to calm me down. "I know that you're nervous about showing Coach your routines, but *now* is the time to focus on your events. You only have a few practices left before Regionals and you can't afford to lose this entire day. Pretend like you're at a meet right now and that . . . hmmm." She stops, tapping her chin with her index finger while she thinks. "Imagine that Coach is one of your rivals, trying to psych you out. Sarah Walker, maybe. You can work on erasing Sarah Walker's meanness by erasing Coach Angelo's presence from the gym today. This is a good opportunity for you, really! It's going to help you get ready for Regionals."

I stare at Maureen like she's mental.

"Don't look at me like that, Joey. I'm just trying to help."

I don't say anything. Instead I chalk up and jump to the high bar again, swinging back and forth until I have enough momentum to do a kip and work on my cast handstand.

"Come on, Joey," Trish says from the set of uneven bars next to mine.

Focus on Trish, not on Coach, I tell myself, and things go a little better as I swing between bars, my release moves fluid and spot on. This time, I stick my landing and lift my arms over my head.

"Joey!" Coach barks again.

What now?

"If your routine gets any more sluggish, the judges won't need to review it in slow motion, because you're already performing in slow motion!"

Trish gives me a look of sympathy.

But I chalk up and do it again.

The minute hand ticks toward 6 P.M.

The moment of reckoning finally arrives.

And then Alex shows up to talk to Coach Angelo about quitting.

Yup. As the clock strikes six, right *after* Maureen has informed Coach that we — as in Maureen and I — have something to show him, Alex calls out from the doorway in a rather timid voice for her: "Coach Angelo?"

The chatter in the gym hushes to silence. Everyone stops what they are doing and turns to look at her.

Alex is standing in the visitor's entrance, not the one that the team uses in back by our cubbies. From this alone, Coach has to know what's coming.

But I think he might be in denial, because he seems happy and *relieved* to see her. "Alex!" he exclaims, then he rushes — he definitely does not storm — to where she is, half-hidden behind the door.

"There's something I need to tell you," she says as he approaches.

The entire team is frozen.

We all knew this day would happen, and now it's here.

The Gansett Stars are about to lose our current Darling.

Before Coach reaches Alex, she shoots me a look, probably hoping for a thumbs-up and a *you can do it* kind of silent support. She's not only done what I've asked of her — waiting until after practice is over to break the news — but she's done me one better, which is to tell him after a Saturday practice, which gives him well over a day and a half to cool down.

My expression, though, probably reads *I am totally panicked by your presence here at this moment!* I can't believe this bad luck, that she showed up right when *I* was going break *my* scary news to him.

Her face falls. She's confused by my reaction. And probably already terrified about talking to Coach on top of it.

See, this is the problem with gymnasts: We are so accustomed to seeing each other for hours and hours at a time during practice that we don't relate like normal girls our age, calling each other up or texting every tidbit of gossip in our lives. So when our communication at practice breaks down because, say, one of us stops showing up, then we're hopelessly lost about how to convey information to each other.

This is a disaster. Not only am I letting Alex down, my heart is pounding so hard I'll never be able to stick my new beam routine for Coach, or even hear the music on floor.

Coach and Alex disappear through the doorway. Even though technically I *do* know what they are talking about, I wish I could overhear what they're saying so I'd have a better sense of Coach's mood and what I'm in for when he has his *next* confessional appointment. With me.

"Joey, calm down," Maureen says, hustling over to where I'm pacing back and forth on one of the low beams. "It's going to be okay."

"Is it?" I ask, because I am not at all reassured that it will be.

I am aware of every round of the minute hand on the gym clock, and it is 6:34 by the time Coach reenters the gym, looking like a person whose puppy was just kidnapped.

"Maureen," I groan.

"Let me handle it," she says, jogging off toward Coach. "Angelo!"

"This is not a good time," he says.

This doesn't stop Maureen. "It's important."

He shakes his head like he is angry or frustrated or annoyed or all three. They talk, their voices so low I can't hear a thing from where I stand on the low beam. I'm afraid to move, though, so I stay put and watch.

Maureen raises her right hand animatedly, waving it around while she talks, first with some subtlety. When Coach responds with a few words, she waves the hand with more agitation. Their back-and-forth continues, with Coach's face growing angrier and angrier, and Maureen's hands becoming wilder and wilder, until she is throwing them way above her head.

This is not good.

Coach suddenly breaks away from their conversation and storms across the gym toward me.

"Angelo!" Maureen calls out, running after him.

But he arrives at the practice beams before she does.

"Joey Jordan," he says, everything about him fuming.

I breathe deep, in and out. "Yes, Coach."

"Don't *yes, Coach* me," he spits.

"Angelo!" Maureen says, joining us.

But he won't look at her. He's staring at me. He closes his eyes a moment and now it's his turn to take a deep breath and let it out.

"Did you know Alex was quitting?" he asks.

Wow. This is not what I expected.

"I can't believe you, Angelo," Maureen says with disgust.

"Did you?" Coach demands again.

I open my mouth, close it, then open it again. "Well, I suspected for a while, and then a few days ago, she told me for sure."

"And it didn't occur to you to tell me?"

Maureen steps between us. "It's not her *job* to tell you. It's Alex's business to make those decisions." She has her hands on her hips now. "And can we please focus on Joey here? Her talent is wasted on those routines you have her doing. I'm begging you to watch these new ones!"

I wish I knew what to do, what to say, how to make this situation okay, but I don't. Coach steps aside so Maureen is no longer between us. "Joey Jordan," he says, using my full name again, which is never a good sign. "You will forget about whatever stunt you've pulled with Maureen this summer, and you will be ready to do your *real* routines at Regionals on Wednesday. You will have your head in the game, and *you will win*. I don't want to hear another word about new routines again. Do you understand me?"

"Yes, Coach," I say in a small voice.

Maureen sighs with exasperation.

"Now you get home and I do not want you to step foot in this gym again before Regionals. I will see you there."

"But —" I try to protest.

"Don't you dare argue. You're lucky you're going to Regionals at all."

"Yes, Coach," I say, even though I'm already wondering if there is anything else I can do or say to convince him before Wednesday. Maybe there is still time. I need to think. I watch as Coach turns, storming off yet again, with Maureen on his heels, arguing the entire way.

Well, at least I'm still alive.

Later that night, I flop facedown on my bed, my mind on overdrive as I try to figure out what to do about this afternoon's disaster with Coach. Then I sense another presence in the room and turn my head toward the door.

Julia's standing there. "Maureen called and told me the news."

"I don't want to talk about it," I mumble.

"It's going to be okay," she says.

"How do you figure that?"

"You'll just do the routines anyway, like we discussed the other night."

"Yeah, and then totally blow my chances of finishing the rest of the events when Coach kicks me out for blatant disobedience."

"He'll calm down."

Julia's obviously not going anywhere, so I flip over, propping myself up with pillows. "Excuse me, but have you lost your memory of what he's like?" I ask.

My sister doesn't answer. Julia is covering her mouth with her hand and staring at the wall. Her eyes are wide with surprise. She's looking at the poster I put up of her, right next to Nadia.

"How long has *that* been there?" Julia asks.

"I don't know. A while," I say, reddening. I don't know why I feel embarrassed that my sister has seen the poster, but I am. A little bit.

"I didn't even know you had one."

"Um, it's been in storage." That's not exactly true, but it's close enough.

"You put it next to all your favorites," she says. "The goddesses of gymnastics."

I roll my eyes. "Don't go getting a big head about it."

"I'm *not*."

"It's not a big deal."

"I didn't say it was."

"Then why did you get all gaspy and stopping in your tracks and all that?"

"I was just surprised. That, and I haven't seen one of those posters in a long, long time. It brings back memories." Julia sounds all wistful as she sits down on the bed.

So I change the subject. "You were saying, about Coach and Regionals? You know, before you got distracted by yourself?"

Now it's Julia's turn to roll her eyes. "I was *saying* that I think you should do the new routines regardless of Coach. Maureen's your coach too."

"I know. But she doesn't call the shots. I wish she did, but Angelo always has the final word."

"Maureen told me that she's going to talk to him again," Julia says. "Try to convince him."

I give my sister a look. "Yeah, well, I wish her good luck with that. Angelo was not exactly happy that Maureen went behind his back either."

"Don't underestimate Maureen. She's been through it all. She has ways of making things happen." Julia seems like she's lost in a memory for moment. "We'll see, I guess," she says. Then: "And I was thinking . . ."

"Uh-oh. What were you thinking?"

"That if you felt okay about it, I might try to talk to Angelo myself."

My eyes open wide. "You?"

"I still have some clout with Coach."

Of course she does. She's the Gansett Stars former Darling. "You'd be willing to do that for me?"

"I would, actually," she says with a self-satisfied smile.

"Well, I'm glad my misfortune gives you a chance to feel good about yourself."

"Joey! I'm just trying to help. Besides," she goes on, "Coach might listen to me, since he doesn't *know* that I was right there with you and Maureen every Friday."

"I know. Sorry," I say. "It's a nice idea but you don't have to do that."

"I have a stake in your success too, you know. I didn't give up all my Friday nights this summer for nothing. I want to watch you win on Wednesday."

"Well, I want to win too."

Julia smiles. "Good."

There's something else, though, something important that's been bothering me and I need to get it out. "But *I'm* thinking . . ." I begin, hesitant at first.

"Uh-oh," Julia says. "Tell me."

"I'm thinking that if I truly want to be a winner, if I'm going to have enough confidence to do this at Regionals, that maybe *I* need to be the one to convince Coach."

"Joey, that might not be the best —"

But I don't let her finish. "You know, I wonder if I might even have a better chance at talking to Angelo, since ultimately, this is between me and him, and I know he's seen the improvement in me lately. He wants the Gansett Stars to win at Regionals just as much as I do. And listen, as much as I appreciate that you care, I think this part is up to me to fix. In the end, these are *my* routines, this is *my* shot at Regionals, and this is *my* gymnastics career we're talking about. So I should take responsibility for it myself, you know?"

Julia's eyes are shiny. "I do know, Joey. I really do."

I purse my lips, not quite knowing what to do in response to all this sisterly affection, but her tears remind me of something I've been wanting to ask her forever. "Julia, when you got the gold medal at Nationals, when you cried up there, were the tears for real?"

She seems startled by my question at first, then falls silent, thinking a while. "Oh yeah. Definitely."

"What made you cry?"

She pauses again before answering. "Wow. It's more like, what didn't? I'd just achieved a lifelong dream, and I almost couldn't believe it, I was so happy. But it was bittersweet too. Because I knew I was going to retire, even if no one else did yet, and it was really hitting me in that moment that my life as a gymnast was ending. Then it's almost like all those times you watch people on television when they're getting the gold, someone drapes the medal around their necks and hands them flowers and they're standing in front of the flag and the national anthem starts playing, and the tears start flowing — it's almost,

I don't know, automatic. You've seen it so many times before but it's never been you, and suddenly now it's *you*." Julia is quiet for a moment. "I could give you about a million other reasons, but that's probably enough."

"Thanks for talking about it," I tell her.

"Sure," she says, getting up from my bed. She glances one last time at the picture on my wall. "Thanks for putting that up, Joey. I hope I'll have one of you up on my wall at college some-day soon, so I can show off my little sister to everyone."

I laugh. "Yeah, I hope that too." She's halfway out the door when I call out to her again. "Julia?"

She turns back. "What's up?"

"I've always thought that if I won the gold at a big meet, you know, like at Regionals, that I wouldn't cry. That I'd probably just smile the whole time. That I'm not the crying type." The truth is, a part of me is worried that this means I'm defective or something, that because I suspect I'd be happy and not teary, that somehow I'm not meant to ever have that experience. Gymnasts are *really* superstitious, after all.

And Julia seems to get that. "Joey, *when* you win at Regionals on Wednesday, and you're up there getting the gold, you'll do whatever feels right. You won't be able to help it. It's just one of those moments of truth in life. And whatever happens, it will be the right thing. Because it's *your* moment and yours only. Just enjoy it."

"Why do you have so much faith in me?"

"You're a natural," she says like this is obvious. "It runs in the family, I think."

I smile. "Maybe it does."

She smiles back. "I *know* it does," she says, and then disappears down the hall.

CHAPTER EIGHTEEN

Give 'em chills, Joey.

The morning of Regionals arrives.

Seriously, it's really here.

I've done a ton of mental prep and my regular beach work-outs, but per Coach's orders, I've yet to go back to the gym. I still haven't figured out how to make him let me do the new routines. But maybe having had some distance between us will make things easier today.

Mom cooks me pasta for breakfast. It's tradition. Jordan girls always eat spaghetti before meets.

"Pasta power!" Dad shouts when he sees me slurping noodles at the table. His saying this is another part of the tradition.

I roll my eyes at him. Also tradition. Before today, though, Mom making me pasta and Dad shouting about it were the extent of their participation in my day of competition. Today, that will change, and this feels good.

Dad sits down in the chair next to mine with a bowl of cereal. "Pasta power!" he shouts again.

I look at him, now scooping up his Special K with gusto. "How am I supposed to get anything down with you yelling at me about my food?" I'm too nervous to say much of anything else. I hope that having a full stomach will help calm the nausea, instead of making it worse.

Dad finishes his bowl and goes in for another. He's about to sit down again when he notices I've just eaten my last forkful of spaghetti. "More?" he asks.

"Okay," I say cautiously.

"Good, because you need all the *PASTA POWER*" — he says this so loud I jump in my seat — "you can get today!"

"Dad!"

"I can't help it, Joey. I'm excited about the meet."

"You're excited?" I want him to say more about this. Also, less about the pasta.

Dad places another heaping dish in front of me and sits down with his second bowl of cereal. "I *am*," he says. "I haven't been to see one of my daughters compete in years. I used to love going."

I stop, surprised, my mouth full of spaghetti. After I swallow it, I say, "You did?"

"Oh yeah. Seeing Julia compete was extraordinary."

"Really?" I've never heard my father talk about watching his daughters do gymnastics as a pleasant thing.

"Of course. Your sister was amazing! But the better she got, the more pressure there was, and the pressure became overwhelming eventually. More so for your mother than for me, to be honest —"

Dad is about to say more but Mom comes in the kitchen. "Did I hear somebody talking about me?" She is dressed in a long, red, flowered skirt that flows to her ankles, and a pale green tank top that makes her look tiny.

"Nope," Dad says quickly, going back to his cereal.

I know the red is Mom's show of support for the Gansett Stars, since it's one of our team colors. I smile, then scoop up a big forkful of my pasta.

"Is it good?" Mom asks me, joining us at the table with her coffee and a book.

"Great, thanks," I say, and we each focus on the task at hand: Mom becoming caffeinated, Dad slurping breakfast, and me getting carbo loaded and trying to calm my anxiety.

Until the doorbell rings.

"Who could that be?" Mom asks, looking up from her reading.

"I'll get it," Dad says cheerfully.

A part of me — maybe more than a tiny part too — wants it to be Tanner. I haven't seen him since we talked on the beach, and I keep trying to forget about him, but it's not easy. It's as though, once I allowed myself to experience the possibility of a me and Tanner who are more than friends, I can't seem to go back.

When my father reappears in the kitchen, he's not alone, but he's not with Tanner either.

Alex is standing there.

"Hey, Joey."

"Hey!" I jump up and run over to give her a hug.

"Well, I'll leave you two girls alone," Dad says and ducks out of the room. Mom follows him, coffee in hand.

Alex says, "I wanted to come by and wish you good luck."

"So you're not coming to watch?" I ask, even though I already know her answer.

She shakes her head. "I want to cheer you on, but I just can't. It's too hard. Too soon. Too sad. You know?"

I nod. It's sad for me too, not competing alongside my best friend for the first time ever in my life, but I understand why she doesn't want to go. "It won't be the same without you, though. I can't imagine you not being there."

"You'll do great," she says. "Don't let Angelo ruin your day, Joey."

"Easier said than done," I say and we both laugh because we both know so well what Coach is like. "But I took your advice, and I've been preparing a speech that's going to make Coach *want* me to do my new routines."

"Go, Joey," Alex whispers, her voice hoarse. "You can do it."

"I know," I whisper back, trying not to get teary. "So I need to get ready. Want to come upstairs?"

Alex hesitates, like she can't decide. "I should probably go."

"Okay," I say, wishing this wasn't so weird, me going off to Regionals while she stays home.

"Good luck," she repeats.

"Thanks."

"Well . . ."

"Yeah," I say, when it's my turn again. "I hope you find something fun to do today. To distract yourself and all."

"I'm going to hang out with Tommy," she says quickly.

"That sounds like a good plan."

Alex leans forward and pulls me into one last hug. "Joey," she says. "You can win. I know you can. Whenever you start to doubt, remember that I'm cheering you on, even if you can't see me."

"I know," I say, unable to stop my eyes from welling up this time.

Why does this have to be so difficult?

"I'm going to go now." She pulls back, her cheeks streaked with tears. "I'll let myself out," she says and disappears through the doorway.

I don't know how long I stand there, sniffling like a crybaby, before my mother finds me. She gives me a mom-consolation, don't-worry-it-will-get-better hug. "That was hard, wasn't it?"

I nod. It's too difficult to speak at the moment.

So we don't. Mom pours me a glass of lemonade and herself another cup of coffee, and we sit there quietly together until my eyes dry up and I've finished my second bowl of spaghetti and things feel like they are going to be okay again.

Mom gets up from the table and futzes around the kitchen, putting dishes in the dishwasher and rinsing out her coffee cup. I get up to rinse my things too, and after I'm done, I turn and see that she's watching me, a weird, excited look on her face.

"There's something I want to show you," she says in a cheery voice and beckons me down the hall toward her studio.

"I should probably get ready. We need to leave soon."

Mom stops, turning around. "It'll just take a sec. Come on."

So I go. I haven't been inside my mother's studio in ages. She's very private about her painting and likes to be left alone until she's ready to do a show. We all know to stay away from that end of the house out of respect for Mom (and also so we don't get yelled at).

Mom halts suddenly at the door and I almost crash into her. She looks at me. She seems nervous.

Uh-oh.

"Ready?" she asks.

"Um, I think so," I say, and we go inside.

At first, I don't notice anything unusual. The studio seems the same as always. Bright and airy, the sunlight filtered by gauzy white curtains, the concrete floor splattered with paint of every color and hue. Drop cloths are draped over the few pieces of furniture; canvases clutter the room, some stacked ten deep in places, others set on easels. A few paintings from Mom's artist friends hang on the walls — she refuses to hang her own in her work space.

I look around, wondering what she wants to show me.

Then I see it.

A painting almost as tall as I am is propped against the wall. There I am in a swirl of color on canvas, smiling from ear to ear, my arms in the air, hands flicked outward, head thrown back as though I'm about to laugh, as if I'm having the time of my life. My legs are outstretched in a perfect split, toes pointed, my body leaping high above the beam, the red stripe on my leotard a bright streak.

"Mom," I exclaim. "I can't believe you did this!"

"Do you like it?"

"I love it," I say, wiping a tear from my eyes because today is clearly a teary day. "How long have you been working on it?"

"Oh, I don't know," she says. "Here and there over the last few months."

This shocks me. *"Months?"*

"More or less."

"You mean, even before I got mad at you?"

My mother puts a hand on her hip and gives me a look. "Joey, have you met me before? Do you really think I could do this in less than two weeks' time?"

I laugh even as tears stream down my face. "I guess not. I just had no idea. I wish I knew you'd been planning this."

Mom comes over and puts an arm around my shoulder and gives me a squeeze. We stand there in silence, admiring her newest piece.

"Mom?"

"Yes, Joey?"

"I'm kind of surprised that you chose to portray me so happy. And on the *beam* too."

Her eyebrows furrow, hearing this. "But isn't beam your favorite?"

"It's kind of a toss-up with floor right now," I say.

"You love beam, though, right?"

"Definitely."

"Then why do you ask?"

"Well, I've always had the impression that whenever you

think of me and gymnastics, all you can picture is me crashing to the ground and hurting myself."

A look of guilt comes over her face. "You heard me say that to Julia?"

I nod.

"Oh, Joey. I'm so sorry. It *is* true that I have a lot of fears about watching you — I'm just so aware that gymnastics is dangerous and that you could injure yourself so easily."

"But I won't," I say.

"I hope you don't, sweetheart."

"If that's what you think about, then what made you paint *this* image of me?"

"I don't *only* think of you falling, Joey. I think of you out there, shining, and giving your whole heart to something you love."

"Really?"

She nods. "Absolutely."

"I'm glad me being a gymnast doesn't *only* make you feel fear, Mom."

"No," she says, looking guilty again. "And even when the fear gets big, I'm going to do my best to get over it, because fear only gets in the way of our dreams, right?"

I laugh. "I've heard that before."

"Me too. From both of my beautiful daughters."

That comment totally deserves an eye roll in this context, so I give Mom one and she laughs.

"I seriously need to get ready," I tell her.

"Go, go. I do too."

I look at the painting one last time and head to my room.

"Pasta power!" Dad yells like a crazy man when I come downstairs, dressed in my team warm-ups, bag over my shoulder.

"Dad, you are *not* allowed to yell that from the stands."

"But if I do, you'll know it's me."

"Dad!"

He changes the subject. "Your mom's in the car and Julia's in the other car, waiting for us. Who would you like to drive with?"

"Julia," I say without hesitation.

"Are you sure? It's a long drive."

"My thoughts exactly," I say.

Dad shuts the door behind us, locks it, and we are off.

If anyone knows what a gymnast's nerves are like on the day of a big competition, my sister does, and so she blares music the entire two-hour ride to the arena where the meet is being held. I appreciate the lack of fake, cheery conversation and the pep talks that would only make me more stressed out.

When we arrive, the parking lot is packed with SUVs and

minivans and people streaming toward the building. But out of all the bazillions of spectators and gymnasts, who walks right in front of our car?

Sarah Walker and Jennifer Adams.

They are so oblivious Julia nearly hits them.

It's almost too bad she didn't. It would have made my day a whole lot easier.

They turn and glare through the windshield, and I feel myself deflate by the time they've moved on. Will I really be able to beat Sarah today?

"Joey," my sister says, turning the music off.

"What?" I ask, like I'm not imploding inside as we drive around looking for an open space.

"You have nothing to fear from those girls. You are a million times better than they are."

I sigh. "Maybe."

She shakes her head. "No *maybe*! You *are*."

"I *am*," I repeat, a smile creeping onto my face. Then I start giggling. Uncontrollably. "I think I might be cracking up from having to face Coach Angelo."

"You'll be okay," Julia says, and pulls into an open parking spot. She turns off the ignition. "And I have something to confess."

"You do?"

"I talked to Angelo last night."

My jaw drops. "But Julia! I told you —"

She doesn't let me finish. "Not about *you*."

"Oh." I wait to hear what she has to say. After a few seconds pass, I'm already impatient. "I can't read your mind! Tell me what happened."

Julia looks smug. She is smiling.

"What?!"

"I went to see Angelo to see if I could work at the gym as an assistant coach, starting next summer."

My jaw drops. "But, Julia! You've always said that you were *done* with gymnastics, as in completely done, which means moving on and *no* coaching. *Your* words."

She looks thoughtful. "That's true. But I may have been a bit hasty in that decision. Something happened that changed my mind."

I wait for her to tell me what exactly. "Which was?"

"Are you really that dense?"

"*Um*, I guess so."

"*Um*," Julia says, mocking me. "Coaching you with Maureen."

"Really?" I am honestly flattered.

"Yes, really. I feel good about it, Joey. Really good."

I watch Julia. She's holding something back. "What aren't you telling me?"

Julia grins sheepishly. "Well, the timing of my talk with Angelo wasn't accidental. I thought maybe I'd butter him up a little before you spoke to him. Between Alex quitting and you going behind his back, and the fact that he's been asking me to coach ever since I retired, I thought it might be good for him to feel like he won *something*."

"Julia! I told you: my career, my responsibility."

"I can't help it! I'm your big sister."

Sighing, I say, "I know. Thanks for caring. And that's really smart, about the winning."

"See? I knew what I was doing. And besides: It's still up to you to make this happen today. Oh, but wait," Julia says. "I have something to give you before you go inside."

"Okay," I say, wondering what it could be.

She rummages through her backseat and pulls out a well-loved and well-worn T-shirt.

I gasp. I know that shirt. Julia was famous for wearing it during her warm-ups. She holds it up so I can read it, even though I already know what it says: Gansett Stars on the front, and I Kick Butt, in big block letters on the back. If I wear it, *everyone* will know who it's from.

"Are you *giving* this to me?" I always loved this shirt, and I wondered what happened to it too. I even went rummaging through her drawers for it one day a while back when she was away at college.

"I am. To give you courage when you talk to Coach. And for luck. It's important to always wear this before a big competition. If you wear it, you can definitely win gold."

I take it from her, the material soft from years of washing. "I guess everyone in our family is feeling generous today."

"Did Mom show you the painting?" Julia asks.

"You knew about it?"

"Well, she showed me after I guilted her about you."

"I got all teary," I confess.

"It's beautiful, isn't it?"

I nod. "I can't believe she made it, after all that resistance."

"Mom's not completely oblivious."

"I guess not," I say.

Julia looks at the clock. "It's time you got in there and started warming up. Show Angelo that you mean business."

I take a deep breath, in and out. Regionals is *here. Help me, Nadia.* I reach for the door handle but Julia stops me. "You can't get out like that!"

"Like what?"

"Put on your shirt. You're going to march in that arena like you own the place."

"What, is the shirt magic or something?" I ask hopefully.

"It is. At least, I always thought so. It never failed me."

"No. I guess it didn't." I take off my warm-up jacket, replacing it with Julia's famous T-shirt. It fits perfectly. "So? How does it make me look?" I twist around so she can see the back.

"Like a girl who's going to go in there and win today."

"Thanks, Julia," I say and give her a big hug.

"Don't thank me. Just *own* those routines."

"Okay."

"And good luck with Coach."

"Okay."

"And one last thing —"

My eyebrows arch, waiting to hear what comes next.

"— give 'em chills, Joey."

I smile. "I'll try."

"There is no try," Julia says.

"Sure thing, Yoda."

Julia puts her hand on my shoulder one last time. "Show the judges the Joey Jordan they've been missing all this time. Make them forget about their jobs."

"I will," I say, and I mean it this time. Then I get out of the car and go inside, psyched up, head held high, ready to kick some serious rival butt.

CHAPTER NINETEEN

So many faces in the crowd.

The arena is huge. Two tiers of seating, the back rows so high and dark I can barely make them out. In the center are the events, the runway for the vault down the entire left side, the floor to the back, the bars next to the start of the runway, and the beam to the right. People are already warming up. A giant scoreboard hangs from the ceiling like an upside-down pyramid. A big college basketball team normally plays here, but today the names of the teams participating in Regionals scroll across the bottom and top in lights.

I watch my competition race by.

WARWICK TITANS

HARTFORD ARIELS

NEWTON TWISTERS

BOSTON GYMNASTICS ACADEMY

VERMONT ELITE GYMNASTS

HANOVER TIGERS

JAMESTOWN GYMCATS

The board may as well say SARAH WALKER over and over again, because she is all I can think about. As the name of each gym appears, there are a few scattered cheers from the spectators filling the stands.

A few more go by before I see

GANSETT STARS

Whistles come from one section in particular, on the bottom tier to my left. Then I hear *"Pasta power!"* and I want to die.

There's a cluster of Gansett Stars parents sitting together. My dad is waving and my mother next to him is chatting with Trish's mom. *My father means well,* I tell myself, and simply wave back. *At least he's here.*

"Nice shirt," says someone walking by.

I remember that I'm wearing Julia's tee. Immediately I straighten, shoulders back, chin up, and walk over to the spot where my team is gathering to begin warm-ups, prancing like I own the place.

I'm ready to talk to Coach.

Coach is nothing if not cool when he sees me.

"Joey," he says, his voice flat.

Stay calm, I tell myself. "Hi, Coach. There's something we need to discuss."

Angelo crosses his arms, the muscles bulging, his jaw set.

I refuse to be intimidated, so I take a deep breath and say the speech I've been working on, with everything that's been swirling around in me for what feels like forever. "Coach, I've been one of your gymnasts for more than half my life," I begin. "And I am grateful for your total devotion to our team and for turning me into the best I can be in this sport — for the fact that you demand no less than this from each of us."

His eyes soften a little — enough that I see. He nods.

"But one of the things you train us to be is independent. We may win as a team, but that win is made up of individual performances. I can cheer for everyone else, but when it's my turn to go up on an event, I go it alone. You've taught me that after I stick something on the low beam, I should know to go up and stick it on the high beam without you having to ask. You've taught me that training in the gym at practice isn't enough, and that to truly make it, I must also train on my own. That to succeed at gymnastics, I am in charge of my own destiny — as my coach, you can only take me so far. But more than all of this, you've taught me to trust my gut when it comes to pushing myself to a new level, one that's beyond everything I've achieved so far."

Almost there, Joey! You can do it.

"And that's where I am now," I say finally. "This summer I knew I was ready for something different, something that would push me like never before, and even though I know you don't agree with what I've done, I hope you realize that without your coaching over the years, I never would have had the confidence to do this, or the independence and motivation to follow it through." Even as the words are coming out of my mouth, I realize that they are true. "And I know, I mean, I *really* know, that today, if you let me do my new routines, they will win me gold."

Coach's arms drop to his sides. "Joey," he says quietly, but that's it.

So I try one last thing. "You demand our trust, Coach. And now I need you to trust me — to trust my gut. Please." I close my eyes.

Wait for the verdict.

Angelo sighs.

The silence feels like it lasts a thousand years.

Then: "I can't believe I'm actually going to say this . . ."

I open one eye, hope beginning to surge inside of me.

". . . but all right, Miss Jordan. I'm going to trust you on this."

Everything about me is suddenly bursting. My heart hammers with joy. "Really?!" I squeal.

"Yes, really," he says.

I throw my arms around him in a huge hug. "Thank you, thank you! You won't be disappointed! I promise!"

Coach lowers me back to the floor. "You'd better win gold."

I'm bouncing, I'm so happy. "I will, I will!"

"Calm down, Joey," he barks suddenly, that familiar demeanor returning in a flash. "You need to focus. You can't win without total focus."

"Absolutely, Coach. Yes, Coach," I say, erasing the glee from my face even though I can't erase the feeling inside, and I run off to find Maureen and tell her the amazing news.

Maureen is thrilled. "That's the best thing I've heard all day!"

"I know! I'm going to make you proud," I tell her.

She squeezes my shoulder. "You will. I know it too."

"I feel like a winner today," I say, then smile big.

"There's my girl," she says, then, "All right, time to go warm up on bars."

"Sure thing." I slip out of my warm-up pants.

I'm ready. Really and truly. I know I am. I jog over to chalk up and meet Trish.

"Joey," she practically squeals, looking around the arena. "I can't believe we're finally here!"

"I know! This is the biggest meet so far in our careers."

We hug, careful not to leave white handprints on each other's backs.

The crowd is growing bigger and bigger every minute. Gymnasts are warming up everywhere I look. With Regionals about to begin, I know that this is the moment I've been waiting for — that I've been *training* for — all summer. A part of me wants to implode with the pressure, with the way this place and its occupants are practically designed to intimidate me, to psych me out, to separate the gymnasts who can from the gymnasts who cave.

But the part of me that is strong, that can withstand it all, is so much bigger.

And I remember the faith that people have shown in me today — my mother's painting, Dad's corny enthusiasm, the work that Maureen and Julia put in to get me here and give me new routines, ones that are especially for my kind of talent. And Coach being willing to trust me. Plus the work that *I* put in to get *myself* to this place.

Because in the end, nobody else could get me here today, but *me*.

This is exactly what I am thinking when Sarah Walker stalks up to us, smirking.

"So, Joey," she says, her voice so sugary I might be sick. She cocks her head to the side. "Do you actually think those sweet little moves you've learned on beam are going to wow the judges today?"

I smirk back. "Gee, Sarah," I say, my tone mocking hers. "Did you walk all the way over here just to reveal your insecurities to me? How thoughtful."

Sarah's expression is haughty. "You can tell yourself whatever you want, Jordan."

"Really? Well, thanks so much," I say, and whirl around so she can see the back of my shirt. "Can you read that, Sarah? Or are the words too confusing?" As I turn to face her again, I clap the chalk from my hands, creating a cloud of white.

Sarah waves in front of her face and coughs.

I stare at her as the chalk settles. "My sister, Julia Jordan — you know, the U.S. National Champion?" I bat my eyes before continuing. "She gave me her favorite shirt for luck today. Funny how she didn't personalize it with your name for me, hmm? It must be because she doesn't even know you *exist*."

"Whatever," Sarah huffs and stomps off to rejoin her teammates.

Trish looks at me with admiration. "Go, Joey," she says. "Where did that come from?"

I laugh. "I think Alex is here with us in spirit."

"Is she coming to watch?"

I shake my head. "She's still hurting. It's too soon."

Trish nods. "Well, we have our own personal cheering section over there anyway," she says, pointing toward where our parents are sitting together.

I turn to see them and I'm met with a huge surprise. Not only are Trish's parents there, and my parents, and Julia talking to one of my teammate's older sisters, and dozens of other family members of girls from the Gansett Stars, but standing on the stairway next to their section is someone I definitely didn't expect to be here today.

Tanner Hughes.

He's wearing jeans and a black T-shirt, his hair falling around his face, his thumbs hooked into his pockets.

And he's looking at me.

Just like I imagined it all summer.

Trish starts squealing again. "Isn't that the boy who sometimes waits for you after practice?"

"Um, yes," I say, still not quite believing that he showed up at Regionals. To see *me*. "I guess it is."

Trish and I get in line for the bars, and while we wait, I keep glancing to where Tanner is standing, watching us.

"He is *so* cute," Trish says.

"Oh, believe me, I know," I agree and smile, ear to ear. Then I look over at him again and give a little wave.

He nods his head, smiling back.

And right then, just before it's my turn to launch into my kip cast handstand that I am certain to perform with more momentum than Coach has ever asked for because my blood is racing, I realize something. Even though boys *can* be distracting and fill your life with drama, and mess with your focus and your drive and all that stuff that makes them forbidden in the life of an elite gymnast, *sometimes* they can make you feel like a million dollars, and *sometimes* their presence at a competition can get you even more psyched up instead of out, and *sometimes* that desire you feel to show off what you've got to impress them can really, truly work in your favor.

Of course, I don't have any other times to compare this one to, since this is the first time a boy has ever shown up to watch me.

I'm just making a guess.

Because, at the very least, I know that today is one of those times.

When warm-ups are over, Angelo and Maureen gather us together.

"Today is the day," Coach says, "that you go out there and show everyone that you are the stars I know you to be. I want you to shine brighter than you ever have before." He puts one arm around Maureen to his right and another around my teammate Heather to his left, drawing us closer in. One by one, all of us follow his lead until all our arms are laced together. "We're going to take home plenty of gold," he goes on, looking at each of us individually.

When Angelo gets to me, he stops, eyes on mine, and nods. I've trained with Coach long enough to know that this is his way of letting me know that he has faith in me. That he *more* than has faith in me. That he expects me to win. That today is *my* day to win.

So I smile back.

"Make me proud today, ladies," he says.

"Yes, Coach," we respond in unison.

"Okay, ready?" he asks us. "One . . . two . . . three . . ."

And my teammates and I all yell together, "Gansett Stars!" and then clap and whistle and cheer as we pull out of our huddle.

Maureen passes around a mirror, then comes around to dab our lips with gloss and brush eye shadow and blush on our faces. Then each of us receives a bouquet of red roses to carry when we march out onto the floor.

The announcer comes over the speakers, her voice booming throughout the arena. "Welcome, ladies and gentlemen, and gymnasts from all over the northeast, to today's main event, the New England Regional Championship!"

The crowd cheers.

My heart leaps in my chest. I look around at the stands, find my parents, my sister, Tanner, so many people here for me today, and smile. Then I take a deep breath, line up behind Trish, and tuck my bouquet along the length of my right arm, gripping the ends of the stems tightly in my hand, the sweet scent of the roses reminding me of all the other times I've done this, gotten psyched up to step out there and present myself to the judges and all those spectators.

Today, everyone is going to go home remembering *my* name, Joey Jordan, gold medal champion. It's up to me to make this happen, and I will. I know it.

"Good luck, Trish," I whisper as we wait for the announcer.

"Good luck, Joey," she says, whispering over her shoulder.

And then it's time.

"Gansett Stars!" booms throughout the arena, and one by

one my teammates and I begin our march, arms swinging, the flowers swishing as we move. Our hands are flicked, toes pointed, chins up, shoulders thrown back, and we wear the biggest smiles on our faces we can manage. We line up one by one in our team's spot on the floor exercise, surveying our competition, acknowledging the judges, then we wave at the crowd with our left hands. When the cheering dies down after the final team is announced, the arena hushes with anticipation.

Regionals is about to begin.

Standing on the podium to receive a gold medal

is like a dream I'll never forget.

For a few minutes I got to share that space with my heroes —

all the girls who were there before me,

and all the girls who will follow after.

It's amazing, getting to be a part of history like that.

— JULIA JORDAN,

U.S. National Champion

CHAPTER TWENTY

Holy medals, Nadia!

So far, things are going all right.

Just all right. My vault was fine, with a score of 9.15. Bars was fairly good, actually, coming in with a 9.20, and it's possible I'll take bronze, which gives me some confidence that I'm still a real contender for All-Around.

And now everything is about to change. Because I'm up next on floor.

Classical music tinkles from the speakers as Jennifer Adams does a very solid, very standard, very boring floor routine. She doesn't need floor to medal today, though. She's already taking home gold on bars. Sarah Walker has a silver on vault, unless someone else manages to get ahead of her, and this shockingly tiny girl from the Newton Twisters who pulled a Yurchenko lay-out full — *she's* taking home the gold.

Jennifer Adams does her final tumbling pass — a very high front tuck step-out into a round-off back handspring double twist — followed by a couple of steps and a leap, and then she drops dramatically to the floor in a tuck as the music ends. The crowd cheers nicely but not wildly. Another ripple of clapping erupts around the arena as a girl from Vermont Elite dismounts on beam, followed by another as someone else finishes bars.

I'm up.

Maureen leans in and gives me a squeeze. "Remember, Joey: poise and style and flair. Look like you're having the time of your life."

"Okay," I say to Maureen, and take a deep breath. I acknowledge the row of judges and begin my march out onto the floor. Screams of "Go, Joey!" from my teammates echo behind me. I hear a "Yeah, Joey! You can do it!" from Julia and a "We love you, Joey Jordan!" in unison from Mom and Dad. There is polite clapping throughout the rest of the arena, but no more than that.

And why should there be? No one has had any reason to pay attention to Joey Jordan before today. Or even so far today. So far, I am only above average. Like Julia said, I need to show everyone what they've been missing.

I hear one last "Go, Joey!" This one's from Tanner.

And I smile. That was just the thing I needed to hear.

I stop when I get to the far left corner of the mat, right near the white lines marking out the boundaries, and get into the starting pose that Maureen and Julia tweaked until they thought it was finally perfect. I wait for the music to begin.

Then it does. Before I can get any more nervous or any more psyched up for this, my floor routine is happening, and not only happening but practically over. Floor routines go so fast. Between the first bars of my fantastic music and the last, I really do have a blast. I dance and fly like never before, and the smile never leaves my face — not because I want to impress the judges, even though smiles certainly help, but because I am honestly and truly in my element. My leaps soar, my tumbling passes are perfect, my flexibility impresses the crowd, I hit every single hand flick and head nod, and I pose like I am born to do this.

And maybe I am.

When I finish, when I strike that very last pose as the final bars of music die away, everything is hushed around me. . . .

And I hold it. . . .

Then I acknowledge the judges and do the customary wave at the spectators in the stands.

That's when the hush ends, and the crowd erupts into wild cheers.

I mean, they really do. For me, Joey Jordan.

I wave some more.

People are standing up and cheering. A standing ovation.

I come off the floor and Maureen sweeps me up into a hug. Then I hug Trish and the rest of my teammates.

Coach Angelo is smiling too, and waiting for me with a hug. "That routine really suits you," he says.

"Thanks, Coach."

Suddenly there are shouts of "Woooo!" throughout the stands.

The judges have flashed my score up on the board.

For a moment, I feel stunned, and then my entire body is flooded with glee and I let out a squeal. I got a 9.70 on floor! Everyone on my team, including Coach, surrounds me, and I am congratulated again and again.

"Yeah, Joey!" Trish says, giving me a hug.

"Thanks," I tell her.

Coach is actually smiling *big*. "That might get you gold, Jordan," he says. "Now go say hi to your sister quickly and then get back here. You've still got beam left."

"Yes, Coach." I run toward the section where my sister and my parents are waiting for me. Mom is practically sobbing.

"Are you okay?" I ask her, my heart sinking. This is the part that Mom has always hated — the stress and pressure of competition.

"Oh, Joey," she gushes, and kisses me on the cheek. "You were beautiful out there!"

"Hey, kiddo!" Dad says, beaming. "That pasta is really working today."

"Thanks, guys," I say, turning red, relieved that they are happy.

Julia shoves herself in front of them so she can have her turn. She looks solemn.

Uh-oh. Here comes the critique.

But then a smile bursts across her face and she starts jumping up and down. I join her so we're jumping together. "You totally nailed it! You are so taking home gold today!" she is screaming and then we hug. "Now all you need to do is stick beam."

"Yeah. That's all," I say sarcastically.

"Hey," Julia scolds me, but she is smiling. "You have a real shot at winning today."

"I hope you're right."

She leans in and whispers to me, "Um, so the boy is here, huh?"

"Yeah, he is, but I didn't tell him to come. We're friends."

"It's okay, Joey. Really. Who knows? Maybe you can have both gymnastics and boys."

"Thanks for understanding," I say, grateful.

Tanner is waiting patiently to the side. Mom and Dad look at me, at him, and me again.

"We'd better get back to our seats," Dad says. "Julia?" He grabs her by the arm and yanks her back up the stairs with Mom.

"Hey," Tanner says, smiling. "You were incredible out there."

I'm beaming. "Thanks."

"I hope it's okay that I'm here. I just . . . I just wanted to see you do this whole gymnastics thing. And be a supportive, um, friend."

"I'm glad you're here," I admit.

"Really?"

I nod. "But I've got to go. I've still got one event left."

"Beam," he says.

"Yup."

He grins. "Well, stick it and all that."

"I will," I say, and turn away to rejoin my team.

Regionals is almost over.

"With that 9.70 on floor, you need only a 9.60 to take the gold on beam *and* the All-Around," Maureen says as I'm stretching.

"Yup, *only* a 9.60," I say, giving her a look.

"Joey, you can do this."

"I know. I can. I *will*." I am trying to pump myself up, but I'm still nervous. It's hard not to be. I stand up, stretch my wrists by pressing them back and forth with my free hand, roll my ankles, flex, and point my feet a few times. Peel off my warm-ups.

The announcer calls my name.

Here we go again.

"Yeah, Joey!" Trish says, giving me a hug.

"Stay tight," Maureen says, with another hug.

"Stick it, Joey," my teammates call out.

I walk over to the beam area. Acknowledge the judges.

My eyes lock with Sarah Walker's. She's standing right behind the judges' table, smirking.

And you know what? Every other time Sarah has done this, she's managed to psych me out. But not today. I just smile back at her like she's one of my favorite people, a fan, even, and then I turn and focus, ready to mount the beam. All sound, all aware-ness of the crowd, my team, my competition today, the dozens of gymnasts from throughout the northeast, and even the judges — they all fall away. There is only me and the beam and my routine and my total love of this event.

I perform, I prance, I display my hard-won shoulder strength that allows me to do presses to handstands, and straddles that could make an Olympic gymnast jealous, and all the splits and poses that show off my flexibility. I do my pass that made Sarah Walker turn white. I do it all like never before, like I'm not tumbling and tossing myself into the air on a four-inch-wide, four-foot-high beam, but like I'm still on the floor. And when I get to the back handspring, back handspring, back layout, I go for it with all I've got.

And I do it flawlessly.

I land my dismount, stick it like the bottoms of my feet are covered in superglue, and throw my arms behind my head. I stay there a moment before I turn and acknowledge the judges. The crowd is cheering wildly.

Again.

And I know I've done it.

I, Joey Jordan, have just won Regionals with that beam routine.

Holy gold medals, Nadia.

"Go, Joey, woohoo!" Trish cries as I run toward the place where my teammates are clapping and whistling. We jump up and down and hug and scream. After we finally stop and I catch my breath, I turn to my coaches. Maureen has tears rolling down her face and she throws her arms around me.

"I am so proud of you," she whispers in my ear. "That was perfect. I knew you could do it."

"Not without you," I say back. Because it's the truth.

When Maureen releases me, Coach Angelo is standing there, towering above us.

I squeeze my eyes shut, waiting for the verdict. Did he totally hate my new routine?

"Good job, Joey," he says and I open one eye nervously. "You need to watch your toes on those press to handstands, though. Your right foot sometimes twitches a little."

"Thanks, Coach," I say, both eyes open now, relieved that he seems happy. Pleased. "I'll remember that next time."

"Pay attention," he says.

"I am, Coach."

"Not to me, to the scoreboard. They're about to announce your score."

Trish puts an arm around me from my left, and Maureen does the same from my right. We stand there waiting for the official word, and I forget to breathe.

Then the score flashes up, and my entire body tingles.

I got a 9.70 on beam! A 9.70!

Everyone is screaming again. I'm screaming. My teammates are passing me around, giving me hugs.

The announcer's voice booms over the speakers. "It's official. Joey Jordan of the Gansett Stars will take the gold on balance beam, and this moves her up to the number one spot in the All-Around."

"Joey!" someone else is screaming. Someone I know well.

Julia almost knocks me over when she arrives, and there's more screaming and jumping up and down. When we finally calm ourselves, I notice tears streaked across her cheeks.

"I knew you could do it," she says to me, her eyes filling up even more. "I knew this was *your* summer, Joey. And it is."

If I wasn't so happy, I might cry too. But I don't. "Thanks, Julia. For everything you've done for me these last couple of months."

"I'm glad I could be here." She puts her hands on my shoulders. "Now, for the big question of the day."

"What question?"

Her gaze is steady on mine. "Do you think there will be tears when you're up on the podium?"

My face breaks into a smile. "You know, I have no idea, really. I've never been up there, so I guess I'll just have to wait and see what happens."

"And I'll take a million pictures," Julia says with a grin. "So I can immortalize whatever you do and never let you live it down, regardless."

"I think that's fair."

Julia and I laugh at this. We are happy, giddy really. We are together. And we are both champions now. Two Jordan girls who took gold medals in the All-Around at Regionals.

And now I have Nationals to look forward to.

How crazy is that?

Later on, when it's time, I'm a bundle of nerves.

People have been handing me bouquets of flowers for the last hour. I don't know where to put them all. Roses. Daisies. Carnations. More roses. Flowers I don't even know the names for. At one point, while they're announcing the medals for bars, a little girl, maybe nine or ten years old, comes up to me.

"Excuse me, Joey Jordan?" she says nervously. Her hair is in pigtails and she is wearing pink warm-ups with a sparkly swirl along the bottom. She is tiny. Compact. Like an aspiring gymnast needs to be.

"That's me," I tell her.

She smiles and holds up her program and a pen. "Can I have your autograph?"

I practically collapse to the ground with shock. Somebody wants *my* autograph. "Wow, sure. Of course," I say, scribbling my name across the program cover and handing it back to her. "Thanks for asking."

"Good luck at Nationals next year," she says and runs off.

"I saw that," Trish says wryly.

I turn to her. "It's never happened to me before."

"Get used to it."

Then it's medal time. I go up once for floor — I ended up with the silver. And once again for beam — the gold, and that's amazing, standing on the top spot, waving at the crowd. But the moment I've waited for my entire life is the one when they call me up for the All-Around.

"Joey Jordan," the announcer says, "the new, All-Around, New England Regionals champion!"

"Go!" Maureen is saying to me. "That's your cue!"

I'm too excited to march or show grace. I practically skip my way to the podium. I climb to the top and face the crowd, waiting for the head judge to reach me with the medal. Everyone I care about in life is here — well, everyone but Alex, and I know she's here with me in spirit. Mom and Dad have their arms around each other, and when Dad catches my eye, he pumps his fist in the air and makes me laugh. Julia looks like she might burst with pride. Tanner is grinning. Maureen is crying. Even Coach Angelo is beaming.

Nationals, here I come!

I throw my hands up, waving at everyone.

There's that wild cheer from the crowd again.

This is pretty great. I mean, I could seriously get used to this.

The head judge finishes giving the silver to Sarah Walker and stops in front of me.

It's time. It's here.

The moment.

My moment.

I lean forward and she drapes the gold medal around my neck.

"Congratulations, Miss Jordan," she says formally, smiling.

"Thank you," I say.

I stand there, waving again, taking in the crowd, this day, this achievement that I will never forget, the faith from the people I love that helped to get me here, and the dedication and sacrifice this sport requires, and I think to myself, *It's all worth it.*

Gymnasts may not get to have normal lives, but we get to have *this.*

I like it up here. I like it a lot. It feels good. It feels like I belong.

And I don't cry at all while this happens. Not even a single tear.

I just smile really, *really* big.